Twist of Fate

Finding Meaning Through Life's Ups and Downs

JERRY ZIEMER

www.ten16press.com
Waukesha, WI

Edited by Kaitlyn Hein
Cover Design by Kaeley Dunteman

To Julie,
my true love,
and my best friend,
without your keen eye,
silly sense of humor,
amazing patience,
encouragement
and love –
I'd still be writing about
The *Pillsbury Dough Boy*.

Contents

Prologue

If you could turn back the clock, what would you do differently? You've probably been asked that question a thousand times. You've probably wondered what might have turned out differently, if either this, that, or the other thing would have taken a different direction. It's human nature to wonder, to ponder. Have you ever encountered a twist of fate?

Everyone does.

Here are 12 short stories, each approximately 3,500 words. Some are intertwined. Some are random. Some may be funny, and some may be sad. One may actually bring a tear to your eye. They will all have the proverbial 'twist of fate' scenario. Each story has some minor thing that changed someone's life forever.

On one hand, if we could actually predict the future using a crystal ball, there wouldn't be any twists. We'd know our future. We'd know what to do beforehand. On the other hand, we all know that's not really possible.

Or is it?

After all, does anyone really know the future? Just wait and see!

Walter and the
Girl with Red Glasses

The Order

An egg white omelet with swiss cheese and six mushrooms, a half cup of cottage cheese, one piece of crispy-crispy bacon, and raisin toast with mayonnaise.

That was the order. That was it!

Seven years at the Cozy Café in Orchardville, as the assistant short order cook, and I've never seen anything like that before. I've prepared thousands of meals, and I've had some incredible requests. The previous best request was from a guy who wanted two raw eggs in a glass of milk. He also wanted a well-done English muffin topped with hollandaise sauce. I really had to learn more about this new request. I knew it had to be from a girl, because no guy would order just one piece of bacon!

My name is Walter, but all my friends call me Skinny. All, that is, except Mary.

"Walter, I think you should serve this order, I think it would be good for you, and you could use a break." Said Mary, our head waitress. Mary was always trying to set me up with somebody. She's been here since before I started. She's my boss Harold's right hand gal, and she also knows my situation better than anyone. Or, at least, she thinks she does.

I used to be pleasantly plump. Now, I guess, I'm just plain fat, or rather large, all depending on the day. At five-feet six-inches tall and tipping the scale at well over 250 pounds, my description depends on your perspective. If I were a bear, I'd be thin. I wouldn't be able to run fast, but at least I'd look thin. I wear my curly hair fluffy and voluminous, so my head seems to be in better proportion to my body. It helps—at least from my side of the mirror.

Saturday morning, the end of May, and I was supposed to have off today. I was going to chill-out, do some sit-ups, some push-ups, some squats, and some deep knee bends—yeah, right. Harold, called me in because his wife reminded him that today is their 25th wedding anniversary. Why do guys forget things like that? He said his wife was going to get him a crystal ball for his birthday next year. If I had a gorgeous wife like his, I'd never forget my wedding day!

Harold's been married longer than I've been alive. His wife, Kay, is a delightful woman. She helps out here every Friday night. She makes the best deep-fried fish in town. I usually have two or three helpings of her coleslaw.

"Walter, you know you shouldn't eat so much of that. It's not really health food."

She tells me it's loaded with calories, but I don't really care. I love it. People come from as far as Sullivan just for our Friday night fish fry. We close at ten, but we're all here till well after midnight cleaning up. So, Harold has his gorgeous wife, and I can't even find a girl. How does that make any sense?

"Walter, do I smell something burning?" Mary said with her nose all scrunched up.

"Oh my gosh, it's the raisin toast. I'll have new ones done in twenty seconds. Thanks, Mary. I was trying to figure out how to put mayonnaise on toast."

"Walter, you look so nice in your little white chef's hat and apron. I think you should get that meal over to table seven right away." Mary was one for prodding, and she could get a little annoying sometimes, but everybody loved her.

"Yes, Mary, just a sec." I was still spreading mayonnaise.

The Cozy Café only has eight tables and six booths, so it was easy to memorize all the locations, which was good for me. Remembering was never very high on my list of essential activities. Mary said the order went to the girl with the big, red-rimmed glasses and the hair that looks like *Leave it to Beaver's* Mother.

Like I'd know that.

Turns out that today's crowd is from a bike ride on the local River Trail. It's a great trail, 25 miles tip to tip. I walk on it every once in a while. I figure maybe I could lose a little weight doing that, but just a little. I probably should walk on the trail more than once a month, though. The Cozy Cafe is just a block off the trail, and sometimes that's as far as I walk. Those are the good days. The walk's not too far.

The bike club, from over in Broadhead is called, The Sore Bottom Riders. They're doing a half-century ride, which is a 50-mile trip on bicycles. That is absolutely amazing to me. If it doesn't need a starter key, I don't know how in the world it can go 50 miles. Cozy Cafe is right near the midway point for them, and I guess they stopped in for a great meal and the nice ambiance. Harold does a great job of promoting the cafe.

Turns out the egg white omelet was the last order from their group. Mary said there were 30 riders, and I'd better get the omelet order out to the girl with the big, thick, red-rimmed glasses before she fainted. The girl, not Mary. Mary was worried the rest of the group might leave the red-rimmed glasses rider behind. She said if I didn't start hustling, there could be trouble.

Mary's kind of a mother hen that way. Always has been, always will be.

I took off my hairnet, fluffed up my hair, and tried to tighten my apron strings so it'd look like I had a waistline. If I remember right, that's what they call it when there's an indentation between your stomach and the thing right below it. I busted the apron string, so I took off my belt, put it over the apron and drew it two notches tighter. Breathing became somewhat harder, but it did put some color in my face. I think I needed that. Mary was pleased. She thought I looked adorable. Can you believe it? Me, adorable?

I put some parsley on the omelet, along with a little sprig coming out of the cottage cheese, just for some color. They say it's all in the presentation, even here at the Cozy Café. But what can you do with bacon and raisin bread with mayonnaise on it? Off I went to the gal with the huge, thick, red-rimmed glasses at table number seven.

The Girl

"Excuse me, miss, but did you order…"

Good Grief—Holy Mackerel—Shut the Door—WOW!!

The red-rimmed glasses gal was beautiful. Her hair was stunning. Her smile was angelic. She had the whitest teeth I'd ever seen. Her glasses weren't just red, they were Candy Apple Red. She had her napkin tucked into her top, just like I do, most of the time, when someone's watching. She set up her silverware perfectly. Her posture, sitting on those lousy chairs we have, was amazing. She couldn't have been taller than five-feet, three-inches, and she was chunky. My kind of chunky. The beautiful kind of chunky.

She was the real deal.

I darn near dropped the plate onto her lap. Looking into her eyes, I was speechless. I felt like a skinny bear, standing next to a princess. I've never felt less fat or less pleasantly plump in my life. Suddenly, my size seemed normal—like I belonged.

"I really like the added touch of parsley on the omelet, and it looks just like a tiny tree coming out of the cottage cheese. I never would have expected anything like that here."

When she said that I believe her teeth were sparkling and she had a halo over her head.

"Well, we aim to please our customers here at the Cozy Café. I'm glad you like it." I was trying to keep my composure, trying to stand straight and make sense.

"And, who thought of the powdered sugar on the bacon? Good grief!" She was too polite.

"Well, that was all my idea. You like it?" I had thought it was another one of my stupid ideas. Ain't life grand?

"Are you kidding? I love it." Yes, she was too polite.

"My name is Skinny, no, no, no, I mean, Walter. My real name is Walter. My friends just call me Skinny. You probably figured that out." I could feel my arms getting rather weak, and some perspiration coming on, but I was all smiles.

"Well, I think it's a cute nickname. My name is Heidi, and you must be an incredibly good cook to have such a fancy outfit. This is the first time I've ever been here, and it's so close to my house. I've got to come here more often." I was beginning to believe her.

Her name is Heidi, and it actually did seem like I heard music when she said her name. She liked my nickname. Some folks think it's derogatory. Just ask my mom. I wasn't so sure what she meant about my outfit, but at least my pants didn't fall down. I was totally tongue-tied, but I did manage a few pleasantries.

"Well, I can guarantee you, you'd always be welcome here. You can count on that. We don't get many single young ladies like you in here. It's usually families or couples, and nobody ever asked for just one piece of bacon before. I thought that was really cool."

Boy, I thought I really messed that up. How did I know if she was single? What in the world did I mean with, 'Young ladies like you?' Does she think I think she's fat? Look at me. Who am I to talk? What's with my brain? Maybe she has a significant other. Maybe she has kids. Maybe she's a nun. Maybe she, maybe this, maybe that, and then again—maybe?

"Have you ever thought about biking? Our bike club could always use more members, and I think you'd fit in just fine. I certainly seem to." That's what Heidi said; however, I had my doubts.

"It'd have to have a motor that I could start with a key just to keep up with anybody." Now the conversation was becoming fun.

"That's sooo funny. I'm sorry I was the last one here, I need more practice in order to keep up with the others. This is my first-time riding in almost ten years. I know I'll never make the whole trip, but I do have to try. Don't I?"

She looked like an angel sitting in our Café.

"You're absolutely right. Maybe I'd try someday, but right now I'd better get back to the kitchen. It was a pleasure meeting you." I smiled.

"No, no, the pleasure was all mine. I love this little cafe, and all the food looks so good. I hope to see you again sometime." My right foot was beginning to fall asleep; I didn't want to fall, and I grabbed onto a chair.

She loved my presentation, the food, and the uniform. She belongs to The Sore Bottom Riders. She invited me to bike with her. What a hoot. What a sense of humor. It was sensational. We were both laughing. What fun.

"Walter, you do know there are other customers wondering about their food, don't you? Or, do you want me to call in Harold?"

Good old Mary. Always on top of things.

"Geeze, yeah. Sorry Mary. I'm right on it." I gave Mary that 'can't you see I'm busy?' look.

"Heidi, I've got to go. Others await my charm. I sure do hope to see you again soon. Bye."

What the heck was that all about, 'others await my charm,' am I crazy? What could she possibly be thinking? Does she think I'm arrogant, conceited, or just plain old stupid? Probably the stupid part. Mary asked me what I was thinking, I told her I wasn't thinking at all. I momentarily forgot all about the café, the grill, my job, doing sit-ups, push-ups, just about everything, except Candy Apple Red.

I was back at the grill doing my thing when Heidi left. I smiled and waved. She smiled and waved back. I thought she blew me a kiss, but that might have been my imagination. No, it must have been my imagination. Yep, only in my dreams.

Heidi's Story

Ever since the fifth grade, this was my normal weekday morning prep for grade school:

"Heidi, honey, it's almost time for school, and laying around in bed won't help you get rid of any of that extra weight." Those were always the first human words I'd hear.

"Mom. It's just 6:30 in the morning, and what do you mean, 'extra weight'?" That was the first sound out of my mouth.

Then the second voice I'd hear. I figured someday I'd miss this routine, but for now, it was becoming a daily weekday game.

"Hey Heidi, it really is time to get up for school. Did you want anything for breakfast today?".

"Daaaaad. It's just quarter to seven, and school doesn't start till eight. You know very well I want something for breakfast." He always knew, it was just 'our game.'

That was normal. Except for Wednesdays! That was the day my Aunt Irene came over to make breakfast. She lived next door and was the head baker at Fran's Sweet Treat Bakery, down on Main Street. Wednesday was her day off, the only one all week. It was my favorite day of the week, hands down.

I'd be up and out of bed, dressed and salivating, long before she got to the house. Aunt Irene made the kind of breakfast I would dream about. The kind you'd see pictures of in those gourmet food magazines. In seventh and eighth grade, I used to cut out pictures of gourmet breakfasts and tape them onto my bathroom mirror. I used to spend more time looking at those pictures than I ever did working on my hair.

"Heidi, what would you like for breakfast tomorrow? What sounds good to you? What's your favorite?" Aunt Irene would sometimes ask me that on Tuesday evening. Those were the hardest nights to fall asleep.

"Aunt Irene, are you kidding? Favorite? How could I pick a favorite? Have you seen me lately? Have you seen my size? Whatever you make, I simply devour. There's no such thing as favorite, not for me." Aunt Irene knew me like the back of her hand.

"Well then, I'll surprise you."

Those were the really hard nights. All I could think about was, "what am I going to feast on tomorrow morning?" Whatever Aunt Irene made; it was always incredible. She made the most scrumptious eggs benedict I've ever had. Her scrambled eggs with bacon-wrapped asparagus spears were amazing. The incredible waffles with her home-made maple syrup were to die for. Everything just seemed to melt in your mouth, and her French toast, there were no words to describe it.

Then she would always finish it off with the most delicious vanilla cream cheese filled coffee cake in the entire world. And her presentation was always as fine or better than anything in those magazines. Wow! Good old Aunt Irene.

I was of normal size when I was born, so I'm told. My folks are both normal, at least in size. My little sister Jan is actually petite. My girlfriends always asked me what happened. I believe I may have a sweet tooth. I'm single, much to Mom's disappointment, but so what? I suppose I should slap my mouth for saying that, but I'm not going to. I'm only 22, I have loads of friends and two jobs. So, what's the big deal?

My sweet tooth probably started on Halloween when I was eight. "Ok, kids. Put all your candy in this bowl. We have to get rid of it all." That's what Mom said when we got home.

"Huh? Get rid of it. We just walked for two hours in our costumes getting it and you want us to get rid of it? Surely you jest." That was my reply.

"No, no, no. Mrs. Jenkins found a needle in one of their chocolate bars and we can't take any chances with our stuff. We've got to toss it all out, now put it in here, all of it." Mom was the greatest, she just didn't understand me.

"Yes, Mother dearest, anything you say." Like heck I was going to give in, my brother could do whatever he wanted. Not me. One lousy candy bar, and it was way over on the other side of town. So, I got up at two the next morning and pigged out. When Mom found out, she was furious. She said I'd throw up and be sick for weeks. I never felt better. I was hooked. I've loved sweets from that day on!

It didn't help that my best friend Kate's dad was a candy sales-man at the local chocolate plant. He'd pay us with candy bars whenever we cut his grass or shoveled his sidewalk. I think I used to pray for rain to make the grass grow, or for snow to shovel. I found more ways to get my grubby little hands on anything sweet than you could ever imagine. I knew I was gaining a little weight, but no one ever laughed at me. I felt fine all the way through high school, and there's always my Aunt Irene. She's no Twiggy, but she's one of the happiest people I know. So, what really was the big deal?

Along with my full-time receptionist job at the chocolate com-pany, I have a part-time job at the Happy Pet, Happy Life, doggie daycare center. Those two jobs keep me plenty active. I have to keep up with anywhere from 10 to 16 dogs every other day for half an hour. I started running (or trotting) with the dogs, for at least the length of the outside kennel. It must be at least 100 feet, so three times that is the length of a football field. I'm told that's good, at least for starters.

I suppose this 'extra poundage,' as Kate calls it, does bother me a little. I'd like to go on dates. They sound like fun! I'd like to look in the mirror and think, how nice, rather than, does anyone else really care? I'd like to be able to run those 100 yards with the dogs all at one time, and all on the same day. The dogs would be happier. I might be slimmer.

Kate picked up her dog this afternoon and we had a short conversation.

"Heidi, you know I belong to The Sore Bottom Riders. Well, we're doing a bike ride next Saturday on the River Trail. You should join us. I think you'd have a ball and it'd get you away from these dogs for a day." Words right out of my dear friend Kate's mouth.

"Kate, it's been so long I'm not sure I remember how to ride. Besides, I'd be a drag on you and the whole club." I was really thinking about myself.

"Nonsense, once you've ridden a bike you never forget how. Besides it would be good for you. Think about how much fun it could be, and you'd never be a drag on me." My best friend Kate, what a chum.

"Fun? Really? Look at me. I'm somewhat on the large size." That was somewhat of an understatement, but Kate is a great friend, she understood. I thought.

"Dang it, Heidi, you've been complaining to me for years about your size. Now, gosh darn it, do something about it." Kate really hollered at me; she is a great friend.

"You're probably right. What's that old Nike saying—'Just do it.' Maybe it would be fun."

I tried to believe her, so I went out the very next day and bought a brand new 18 speed red beauty, with all the bells and whistles. I'm going to join them, I'm going to 'Just do it.' I'll put on my big, neat, red-rimmed glasses, and who knows?

I figured, what did I have to lose?

Back at the Café

For the next few weeks, I couldn't get Heidi out of my mind. I wondered, how could anybody like that not have a significant other? How could she possibly fall for someone who looks like the Pillsbury Dough Boy with a curly mop of hair? What are my chances of ever finding a soul mate?

I spent a lot of time struggling with those questions.

I asked my boss for all the extra hours he could spare, just to take my mind off of Little Red. That's what I started calling her. Mary got mad at me. She kept telling me to grow up. Like that's what I needed to hear. I thought I'd grown a little too up. Maybe I should grow a little down. Maybe if I dropped 50 pounds. Maybe if I shaved my head. Maybe if I did those sit-ups and push-ups.

Maybe this, maybe that, maybe something else, and then again—maybe?

I paid a visit to The Sore Bottom Riders at their monthly meeting two months later. I talked to a couple of guys that were standing around the water cooler. They had those Spandex outfits on that you see riders wearing. They gave me a funny look, and I figured they were trying to envision me in Spandex. Not a very pleasant sight. I'm not sure what they noticed more, the beads of sweat coming off my forehead, or the fact that I kept stuttering. I didn't see Little Red anyplace, so I calmed down somewhat.

"Hey, you guys were on a bike ride a couple months ago, and you stopped at the Cozy Café for lunch. I'm Walter and I'm a cook over there. It looked like you were having lots of fun."

When I mentioned I was from the Cozy Café, one of the gals at the front table giggled. I wondered what Heidi might have told her about me or was the gal just trying to picture me in one of those spandex outfits. I believe I may have passed a little gas. I'm not sure. I did, however, feel my face getting warm. I was starting to get a little panicky and needed some fresh air.

I picked up a membership application, smiled, shook a few hands, told them I thought I could use a little more exercise, and I left. I was too nervous to ask about Heidi. I guess I was afraid someone might tell her I stopped by. Maybe she has a significant other. Maybe she'll think I'm stalking her. Maybe she'll never want to see me again. Me and those damn maybe's. However, I did make an inroad with The Sore Bottom Riders.

I'll go back. I'm going to get to know Heidi, and with any luck she's going to become my angel with the Candy Apple Red glasses.

WHAT IF – Walters boss Harold, hadn't called Walter into work?

Betty the Bowler
& Her Cowboy

"Get your ball out there, just past the arrow. Hit the third board from the right gutter, not the second board, and definitely not the fourth board. It'll be a thing of beauty, just you watch. It'll dive into the pocket, and the pins will explode." That's precisely what Charlie, my bowling instructor and the man I call Grandpa, told me that Friday night—November 19, 1970.

So, what did I do? I swung the ball right over the sixth board. It wasn't a thing of beauty, as a matter of fact it stunk. My ball caught the oil buildup created from an evening of bowling and skidded halfway down the alley. It straightened out and hit the six-pin head on. I wound up getting the six, nine, and ten pins. I left seven pins. I'll never learn.

"Grandpa Charlie, I trust you, you've been teaching bowling for over 30 years. You and Grandma Betty have a warehouse full of trophies. I've got complete confidence in what you're telling me to do, but it just isn't all that easy." I was totally frustrated.

"Suzy, if it was easy, I'd be out of a job. You've got to trust me. You know, Trust is a Must."

Trust? What's Charlie talking about? Trust who? Trust what? That's what I was thinking. Sure, I trusted Charlie, but that's a far cry from, well—you know what I'm talking about. Right?

Grandma Betty

She was quite the bowler back in 1952, she was also my grand-mother. I called her Grandma Betty and she called me Sweet Suzy Q. Naturally, she was from my mother's side of the family. I'm not sure I ever saw anyone from dad's side of the family walk a straight line. But that's another issue.

I was just 9 years old back on that day. It happened on Saturday, May 24, 1952, sometime around five in the evening, and I was a witness to it. It left a lot of us speechless. I don't think I ever heard the bowling alley so quiet, as a matter of fact, you could have heard one pin drop. In the background, someone started the song "Tell Me Why" by the Four Aces on the jukebox.

Grandma Betty's teammates started shouting, they were all around me. I was sitting on the front chair right next to the ball return. I was Grandma's pet, she always referred to me as her 'lucky charm.' The other team just stood there with their mouths wide open. No one knew what to do. It seemed as though everything was frozen in time. I believe it was a moment when time actually did stand still.

Her Story

Grandma started bowling when she was 12 years old, at least that's what she always told me. She said there was a boy in school named Frederick. He was one year ahead of her, and he loved bowling. She told me he was 'hot stuff,' and she was going to get him to notice her. That's one of the things I loved about Grandma Betty, she was a pistol. A feisty pistol.

According to her they bowled a lot together, but she NEVER let herself beat him. She was a true lady back then, that was in

1917. Grandma lost touch with Frederick when he went off to college, she thought it was a good thing. Grandma was tired of throwing gutter balls just so he could win. Chalk one up for her. From that time on, absolutely nobody was going to beat her, and not many ever did.

So, there we were, Saturday, May 24, 1952, at Somerset Lanes in Racine, Wisconsin. Grandma's team already had first place locked up, they were in the lead by 150 pins. They were bowling for first place in the Wisconsin State Championship Tournament. The entire team was starting to celebrate, with just one little matter to finish. Grandma had already bowled nine perfect games up to that point in her career, and this might be the tenth. Right there at the State Championship. Wow!

As a bowler, Grandma was fierce. She had a cut-throat demeanor, her eyes were piercing, and she didn't talk much. When the game was over, she was as much fun as the next gal. As my Grandma, she was incredibly sweet and loving. I loved her, and she loved me. What more could a nine-year-old girl want?

It was the last frame of the last game, and Grandma was the last bowler. They call that the 'anchor bowler.' She seemed to be born for that position. There were eleven X's on her score sheet, just one more to go for the perfect game. I was sitting on that front seat, sitting on both my hands with my fingers crossed. Watching that third board that Grandma always aimed for. It was the spot Grandpa Charlie always told her to hit…

Wait a minute, I'm getting ahead of myself—

Elizabeth Immaculata Belado, (aka: my Grandma Betty), was born on January 1, 1900 at precisely 7:11 in the morning. She was not just a New Year's Baby; she was a New Century Baby. She was born at Saint Mary's on The Lake Hospital in Milwaukee, Wisconsin. Grandma was raised in Milwaukee's Third Ward. She was Italian through and through, and she was Catholic. She learned the true meaning of trust in a 'greater power' from the nuns at the Catholic grade school and high school she attended. One of her favorite sayings was always, Trust is a Must.

She met her first husband, Jack, when she was 20, just three days after her birthday. She always told me he was the most charming fellow she ever knew. Grandma was working at the local bowling alley as a waitress when she met Jack. She earned 'pin money,' as she called it, from hustling bowling games.

Jack was a traveling salesman. He sold a complete line of bowling alley equipment, and he swept her off her feet, so she said. They were married six months after meeting each other. My mother was born six months after they married. Jack disappeared two months after my mother was born.

That was Grandma's first bout with trust.

Charles Riding Bull Whitehead was born on January 1, 1900 at precisely 6:30 in the morning. Another New Century Baby, but Charlie was born in Billings, Montana, and he was a cowboy. A true, authentic, born in the USA, Cowboy. His mother was a Blackfoot Indian Princess, and his father was a misplaced Irish Cowboy who taught Charlie everything he knew. Charlie loved bull riding and bowling. He was great at both. Charlie could do whatever he set his mind on, and he wanted to own a bowling alley.

After the stock market crash of 1929, Charlie found a little bowling establishment in Stillwater, Minnesota at a price he couldn't pass up.

It was a 12-alley building with a nice bar, locker rooms, and indoor bathrooms. What a deal. Charlie was thrilled. He loved his new place. He named it, The Bull Stops Here. It was 1930, times were tough, but Charlie was content. Single and content.

In the spring of 1931, Grandma Betty belonged to a group of female bowlers who were touring the Midwest trying to promote bowling. It was an attempt to bring some joy and togetherness for folks around the country, right after the Great Depression. They called themselves 'The Alley Girls.'

One of their stops was supposed to be in Minneapolis, Minnesota, but due to an unforeseen carburetor problem with the bus they were using, they wound up in Stillwater. They found this nice little bowling alley called The Bull Stops Here and decided to have a little fun.

Elizabeth Immaculata Belado met Charles Riding Bull Whitehead on Friday, May 15, 1931 in Stillwater, Minnesota. They were married on Saturday, July 4, 1931 in a small chapel in Stillwater. Grandma became Mrs. Whitehead, and with my mom, moved to Stillwater. Life was good for her and my mother.

Charlie never minded that she could beat him in bowling, and she never had to throw another gutter ball. Charlie called Grandma his 'Little Italian Paleface' and Grandma called Charlie 'Mister Bull,' it was a match made in heaven, at least according to Grandma Betty.

In the summer of 1942, they sold their bowling establishment for a considerable profit and moved back to Milwaukee. Grandma was missing her daughter, her family, and friends and she thought 11 years in Stillwater was just enough. Grandma always said, "Stillwater was a good place to be from."

Mom was 21 by that time and had moved back to Milwaukee three years earlier. I was born three months after Grandma and Char-

lie moved back to Milwaukee. *Grandma gave me little pink bowling shoes for my first birthday. I still have them.*

The Game

So, there it was, Saturday, May 24, 1952 at around five in the evening. I'm sitting on the edge of my seat, on my hands, and with my fingers crossed. One more strike and it'd be Grandma Betty's tenth, 300 game, and done at the Wisconsin State Championship Tournament. All I could think was, "WOW, and I'm a witness to it." Grandma Betty and Sweet Suzy Q, what a team we were.

Grandma put the ball down right over the third board, not the second board, and definitely not the fourth board. Just like Grandpa Charlie had told her for 20 years. It was a perfectly placed ball, right on target. I couldn't have been happier. It was destined to be a solid pocket hit. A bullseye according to Charlie, the pins were going to be flying. A tenth 300 game, and right at the state tournament.

Then, all of a sudden, there was this shrill scream from in back of the alley.

"EYE—YI—YI—YI —YI!"

The pin sweeper slowly started coming down from above. Grandma's ball was just starting to turn in toward the pocket.

It became a slooooooooooooooooooooow—mooooooooootion— moooooooooment!

No one said a thing. Eyes were bulging, people stopped breathing, all you heard was the ball rolling down the alley towards its destiny. Thump, thump, thump. And then, all I heard was SMACK. It was a SMACK that could have been heard across town.

Grandma's ball bounced off the pin sweeper. Up about five feet into the air, and back about 20 feet. It flew across two lanes and landed right in the middle of another lane. Grandma had fallen to her knees and had thrown both hands up into the air when the pin sweeper started coming down. She hollered something, but no one would ever tell me what it meant. When her ball hit the pin sweeper, she fell flat on her face and broke her nose.

It turned out that Jimmy, the owner of the bowling alleys grandson, was in back by the machinery. He often monitored things just in case something went wrong. Well as Grandma's luck would have it, he had gotten an incredibly sharp cramp in his right calf muscle. According to Grandma, Jimmy never was the sharpest knife in the drawer, and he wasn't paying attention to what was going on. His right leg shot straight out like a rocket. His right foot accidently hit the emergency pin sweeper lever, and down came the sweeper. Right in front of Grandma's ball.

Grandma's ball hit the sweeper so hard that it broke the braces on it. It pushed the sweeper all the way to the back of the alley. It knocked down all ten pins. The powers that be eventually figured out that the spot where the ball hit the pin sweeper, was the exact spot where it would have gone in for the perfect pocket hit. They couldn't give Grandma Betty the perfect 300 game, so they counted it as a 299 game.

Grandma Betty never bowled another game after that. She'd had her share of questions about that whole Trust is A Must idea during her lifetime. That might have been the tipping point.

The Home & Betty
"B-10," - Huh? That's how many 300 games I should have bowled!

"O-31," - Huh? That's the year I met Charlie!

"B-41," - Huh? Charlie's 41 minutes older than me!

"O-52," - WOW! That's the year I hit that damn pin sweeper, oh, my gosh - "BINGO!"

"Who said that?"

"I said that."

"Well, who are you?"

"I'm Betty Whitehead, that's who I am." Grandma's back.

"Well, you can't have bingo, and when did you get here?" That's what the young girl running the bingo game at the home asked.

"Well, I do have bingo, and I got here yesterday afternoon. Now why can't I have bingo?" Grandma was getting as feisty as ever.

"Because I only called four numbers." The young girl was new at playing with older residents, she thought she was smarter.

"What about the four corners?" Good old Grandma Betty, sharp as a tack as usual.

"Oh, I forgot about those." That was her introduction to my Grandma Betty back in the summer of 1970. She introduced herself as Kathleen Somers, and said she ran the activities at the lake area branch of the Westfield Care Center. She had no idea what she was in store for.

"What about my prize, what did I win?" Grandma asked.

"Betty, I'm not sure how to tell you this, but we don't actually give out prizes here at Westfield. We feel that just playing the game with the rest of the residents is a prize enough."

That's what Kathleen told Grandma Betty. Boy that was a mistake, but she'll learn.

"HUH? You don't give out prizes, what's the reason to play? I wasn't born yesterday; everybody wants to win something. Don't they?" That was my feisty, feisty grandma.

Grandma didn't know I was coming to visit, so I just stood in the back of the room, listening to the whole conversation. I had a huge smirk on my face. Kathleen saw me, but she had no idea who I was. I'm sure she wondered what I was smiling about.

"Well, Betty, there are other things you can win here, they just aren't things you can touch. You can win love, friendship, happiness, and you can win trust." That's what Kathleen told Grandma Betty. I'm sure she meant well.

"Oh, so you're one of those goody two shoes, aren't you? I know all about your kind." That was Grandma's reply. I felt a little queasy. I figured I'd better introduce myself and do it quick.

"Hello, Kathleen. My name is Susan, and I'm Betty Whitehead's granddaughter. Grandma just got here yesterday afternoon. She's here in rehab because she had a hip replaced three days ago, and no one else wanted her. No, I'm just kidding, I think you understand." I weaseled out of that one, but there was some truth to what I'd said.

"I think I'm beginning to. Are you blood related, or is it just through marriage?" Kathleen was picking up on us.

"I'm proud to say she's my Mother's Mother, and she's a pure, unadulterated Catholic Italian. You probably have no idea what that means, but you'll find out soon enough." I'm not sure why I pushed the Catholic Italian part, possibly because of their incredible sense of pride, faith, and trust.

Grandma Betty was also there because lately she'd been getting a little confused about some things. Her doctor thinks it may go back to that day she fell flat on her face and broke her nose. He thinks she may have suffered a mild concussion, and it may not have shown up until now. I think she's just being Grandma Betty. But Grandma Betty at age 70.

"Well, she certainly is a feisty one. If she's in rehab she won't be here that long, I'll get used to her. Maybe we can even have some fun. That's what I like most about my job. I'm here to entertain the residents, to keep them active."

I was beginning to like this young Kathleen Somers.

From her wheelchair Grandma chimed in, "Will the two of you quit talking about me as though I'm not here. Now, where's my prize? What did I win?"

"Well, Betty, let me see what I can find for you. Here's a neat balloon that says, 'You're the greatest,' how's that?" Kathleen was trying to be nice, but I knew she was asking for it. I thought I'd better intervene.

"Grandma how would like me to take you to your room. It's been a long day and I could push you there. We can visit for a little while, like the old days." I'll never stop loving my Grandma Betty.

"Sounds good, but I don't need to be pushed. I can take care of myself just fine. I'm not dead yet."

Good old feisty Grandma Betty. What a pistol, she hasn't changed since—well, since forever. We all knew she hated being there. There just wasn't anyplace else for her to go. My husband Richard and I certainly didn't have any room, we sold our home and downsized two years ago.

Grandpa Charlie loved her to pieces, but he couldn't take care of her. With her new hip it'd never work out. Grandpa was out of the question, although I really don't think he felt too badly about it. He said it was peaceful at home. I went to visit him that evening.

"Grandpa, it seems as though Grandma hasn't lost any of her feistiness. She's as big a pistol as ever. How on earth have you put up with her? I always thought she was such a sweetie pie." Grandpa

Charlie, my bowling instructor, was as always, warmer, kinder, and more understanding than anyone I'd ever know.

"Honey, you'll never know. Right now, she just needs some pampering. It may sound strange, but ever since that night, she hasn't been the same. Nothing big, just little things." That night seemed to have had a profound effect on her. I hadn't realized it, but Grandpa has had to live with it for the past 18 years.

"Yeah, I think I know what you mean." We were sitting in their little apartment; Grandpa was in his usual chair and I think I saw tears in his eyes. I stayed quiet after that.

"She always seems to be waiting for something to go wrong. Somedays she gets all on edge, like she doesn't trust anything. You were there, you saw it happen. It seems to have changed her, but I still love her." I hugged him and left.

I knew Grandpa Charlie was right. I'd noticed little things also. So now we were just going to pamper her. Have fun with her. Re-develop her trust, and the folks at Westfield were going to help.

I trusted them.

The Recovery

Grandma was released from the Westfield Care Center exactly six months after she entered. Her hip had adjusted fine and she was walking again. She'd use a walker here and there, but she was able to get around on her own with no trouble. She had to do physical therapy once a week for the next three months which she enjoyed; she liked the attention.

Grandpa said her entire disposition had changed when she got back home. He figured that Grandma must have realized how great a life she had after spending six months in the nursing home with the other residents. She saw what obstacles life could really throw at you. She figured out bowling wasn't all there is to life. Grandma finally realized that she'd had a wonderful life, and still had plenty left. I figured it was the Italian Catholic in her.

Grandpa was thrilled. So was I.

Grandma Betty even made him put up two shelves so she could display some of her many trophies. Right in the middle of the entire bunch was the trophy from back on May 24, 1952, and right next to that was the pair of pink baby shoes from my first birthday.

Grandma was inducted into the Women's Bowling Hall of Fame on her 70th birthday. They retired to Hot Springs, Arkansas in 1972, where they can both golf whenever the urge hits.

WHAT IF – The bus hadn't had carburetor trouble and broken down?

The Shrimp, the Bully
& the Billboard

Bernardo Fernando Rapinski was born eight weeks premature at Saint Helen's Hospital yesterday. The doctors and staff are doing their best to keep him stable. Any and all prayers are greatly appreciated by the family. The police are still looking for the driver who ran the stop light on 15th and Main streets. The accident caused the rush to the hospital and the premature birth. Anyone with information is asked to call the police department at 555-4567.

That's how it read in our local newspaper, the day after I was born, 17 years ago.

The Phone Call

I hadn't seen my friend Sammy in a couple weeks, and I wanted to let him know what was happening. He was a crucial part of what was going on, and I wasn't sure how he'd take the news. I would rather have told him in person, but he was out of town for a month, and I sure didn't want someone else telling him, so I gave him a call.

"Hey, Sammy, it's Bernardo. How you doin?" I was thrilled to get ahold of him, even though I was running a little behind schedule.

"Hey, Bernardo. How've you been? I haven't seen you in a while. You doin OK?" He never did like pronouncing the letter 'g.'

"I'm OK. Hey, I've got some interesting news for you. I think it might freak you out!" In all the while I've known him, I never saw anything freak Sammy out, but I thought I'd try.

Sammy and I go back to grade school together in Racine, Wisconsin. I started kindergarten there, and Sammy transferred in the middle of the fifth grade. His father was a branch manager for a national bank in Queens, New York, and was sent to Racine to open a new location. His family thought it was a great job promotion, and it would be an incredible family adventure.

It turned out to be both.

Sammy was Irish, Methodist, and straight from Queens, New York. What a hoot he was! To say he didn't fit in at first would be an understatement. He was taller than most of us, and a little on the stocky side, but just a little. My folks said his complexion was ruddy, like many Irish people. He had long wavy red hair, and a smile that seemed to go from ear to ear.

He was 12 when he came to our school, he had been held back one year in Queens. He said it was because his speech was a little different, but I couldn't tell anything strange, just an accent. When he walked, he always seemed incredibly confident, stood straight up and tall, and had no hesitations. It was like he was in charge of everything, much different than me. When I walked, my shoulders seemed to slump, and I looked down. One day, when I was crossing the playground during fifth grade recess, I overheard Karen and Lynn talking.

"Lynn, did you see that cute guy that started yesterday over in Miss Betty's classroom?" Karen was incredibly excited; I believe she ran to catch up with Lynn.

"Sure did, Karen. How in the world could I miss him? I think he's gorgeous, how about you?" I thought it looked like Karen was ready to faint. I didn't think Sammy was that good looking.

"I agree with you, but I heard that some of the guys are a little jealous of him. They said they thought he was odd because he talks so funny, and he laughs too much. They kind of pick on him." Karen and Lynn formed Sammy's first fan club.

"The way he laughs is one of the coolest things about him. I heard his name is Sammy and he's from New York City. Can you imagine that? He's here, all the way from New York City. Those other guys better be careful. Sammy's a lot bigger than any of them." She was dead on with that comment, but I didn't say a word. I just kept walking.

"Well, I don't care what those guys think, I think he's adorable, and I like the way he talks. He sure doesn't seem to care what those guys think, and neither do I. They're all kind of jerks anyway, all except Bernardo."

Well, I straightened up my shoulders, looked up straight ahead of me, and understood why I liked Sammy right from the start. If I made him laugh, I'd have to stand back, look out, and wait for the howl. I knew it was going to come. That was Sammy. Boy could he laugh! He and I became good friends almost from day one. I think it was because he was new at school, and the other guys picked on him. He wanted a new friend, and he saw my predicament. We were a good fit. I was about four inches shorter than anyone else, including the girls. You could say I was skinny, not thin, just plain old skinny.

I was told being born eight weeks premature can cause that. I never liked that explanation, it always ticked me off. It seemed like a cop-out. I wanted to be normal for a change. That's all I ever wanted, just to be one of the guys.

Most of the kids in school called me Bernie, but whenever Sammy said Bernie it always came out Beanie. He had a hard time with the letter 'r', he said it was because of his accent. After about the fifth day of saying Beanie, and getting totally frustrated, he switched to Pinski, short for Rapinski. That worked out fine with me.

Within three or four weeks, he had almost everybody in school calling me Pinski. My relatives settled in Racine in 1875, so the Rapinski name was well respected. That nickname stayed with me my entire life.

Sammy helped me feel normal. He accepted me for who I was, and he didn't care about my size. I think I was a good sidekick for him. At least that's probably how it started. As short and skinny as I was, it always seemed to me like my brain was bulging out of my head. I could remember everything I read. My teachers said I had a photographic memory. I just thought my brain was way too big for my body.

Between Sammy and me, we made a good team. When I was with Sammy, I felt six inches taller, I even walked straighter. I liked that. School was fun. For once, things were finally looking good for me.

Back to the Call

"Sammy, about my reason for calling you. Do you remember that guy Duke? He started school with us in the seventh grade, and he used to give me a hard time." Sammy and Duke never did hit it off in grade school. They even had a few fights. Sammy never talked about them, but Duke would always grumble about Sammy.

"Hell, yeah, I remember him. How could anybody forget him?

He was way more than a bully to you. He was downright mean to you in grade school."

Sammy remembered. For some reason, Duke and I never got along, he's the one that started calling me 'The Shrimp.' He got a couple of other jerks to use that same nickname.

"Well, I've got some interesting news about him…"

"Pinski, just to let you know, I did have it out with him a couple times. One time I took on him and two of his friends. I figured it was always a good workout. It used to happen to me back in Queens all the time."

Sammy did have a habit of interrupting.

"Well, that's not at all surprising, but about that news…"

"Pinski, back in Queens I was plenty big for my age, and some of the older guys would always try to get my lunch bucket away from me. I always got a kick out of it, but I never lost my lunch bucket."

Sometimes the habit of interrupting could be annoying.

"Yeah, yeah, yeah. But about the news I have in regard to Duke…"

"Pinski, I know Duke was a jerk and all. I also know it took some time for you and him to be civil together, but just try to forget him. You don't ever have to see Duke again after we graduate from High School."

That's the way a lot of my conversations with Sammy went. I always chalked it up to the fact that he was Irish, he liked to talk and talk and talk, and laugh and laugh and laugh!

Duke truly was a bully. I don't know why he acted the way he did around me. Maybe bullies have no reason. I never really did anything to him, and I tried to ignore him as much as I could.

He and a couple of his buddies just kept coming up to me, saying "Shrimpy, Shrimpy, Shrimpy." Or things like, "Hey Shrimp, you live in a different time zone down there?" Or, "Hey Shrimp, you still sleep in a crib?"

Duke transferred to our school in the middle of seventh grade. There were three different rumors about why he was there. The main one was his mom and dad got divorced, and she was from Racine and moved back here with Duke. The second one was his dad was sent to jail for beating her up, and she moved back. The third one, and the one us guys liked the best, was that his mom shot his dad right in his privates, and she moved back to Racine just to get away from him. That was also my favorite, hands down.

One day, Sammy, Frank, Joey, Dick, Nancy, Debbie, and I all got together and did a little play acting out on the school playground. I pretended to be Duke's dad; Sammy pretended to be Duke's Mom trying to shoot off my privates. Frank and Joey made believe they were the cops arresting Duke's Mom. Nancy and Debbie came running over to me, trying to take care of me like nurses would do. Dick made believe he was a TV anchorman trying to interview Duke's mom.

It was incredible. We were all breaking up and in stitches from laughing. The problem was, Sammy was laughing so darn loud, that Duke heard us. He was furious, and he told our teacher, Mrs. Davidson. She thought it was cruel, and then we got into a whole lot of trouble with our principal Mr. Stearns. We all still laugh about it when we see each other.

Duke grew up out in Santa Monica, California, near the Pacific Ocean. None of us guys could figure out why he was always such a jerk. We all thought growing up in California near the ocean would have been fantastic. I guess we never walked in his shoes. He must have been trying to prove something to himself. It just seemed dumb to the rest of us, especially to Sammy.

Duke was almost the same size as Sammy, just not as stocky. Duke had a great California tan and wavy blonde hair. If he wouldn't have been such a jerk, the girls really would have liked him. I believe Sammy was a little jealous, but he had that great Irish laugh, so you could never tell how he felt about some things. He was good at covering things up with a joke and a laugh.

Back, Once Again, to the Call

"Sammy, do you remember that trick we played on Duke and his buddies back in eighth grade? I swear he was almost crying, and his buddies kept saying they didn't even know him. His one friend went so far as to say that he was really my friend, not Duke's."

I wasn't sure if Sammy would remember or not, however the trick was imbedded in my brain for eternity.

"Geeze, how could I forget that. That was one of the best tricks we ever played. Things slowly started to change after that. It was a long, slow process, but maybe that's when Duke realized he really didn't have to be such a jerk." Sammy remembered; I was thrilled.

It was another dumb sort of trick. The kind only eighth grade guys could think of. Sammy and I were going to fake my death. I had five small packets of ketchup. I ran them all around my nose, and I laid down on my back and played dead. Sammy ran over to Duke and his two buddies. We thought this was really going to be good; no, we thought this was going to be great.

We were right.

"Duke, you lousy bum! What did you do to Pinski? I found

41

him lying on the ground over there with blood all over his face. I think he's dead! When the cops get here, I'm telling them you punched him in the nose and killed him." I never thought Duke would actually fall for this.

"Sammy, I didn't do nothing. I don't hate The Shrimp. I just like giving him a hard time." It sounded like Duke was taking the bait. Holy cow!

"Duke, everybody knows how much you hated him. What a bully you've been to him. They'll believe you and your buddies did this. I know they will. By the end of today, you're gonna be in jail, and Pinsky will be in the funeral home." Sammy did have a deep convincing voice; I was all smiles inside.

"You can't pin this on me! No way! My buddies can tell you; I wouldn't kill anybody." I don't think Duke would have, but this was starting to be fun.

Boy, Sammy was good. I had a hard time just lying there listening to him. All I wanted to do was applaud. I could tell Duke was squirming, and then I heard his buddies trying to get away.

"Hey, Duke, keep me out of this. I don't know nothing about you and The Shrimp. I was just walking by the school."

That's what his one buddy said. His other buddy started walking backwards almost running away from us, saying, "I always liked The Shrimp, and he was always nice to me."

I was laying there with one eye slightly open quietly laughing inside, trying not to move.

"Duke, what're you going to do? You going to run away like your buddies? The cops will find you. You can't hide from this. They know where you live." Man, this was fun.

"Sammy, I didn't do it. You know I didn't do it. Is this some kind of dirty, rotten, lousy trick again? I'm getting darn tired of being picked on. I think you're bullying me."

Duke was sweating. Sammy was having a ball. He could have won an Oscar that day.

All of a sudden, I just couldn't take it anymore. I started rolling on the ground and laughing. Sammy started howling, and Duke was pissed. He didn't talk to either of us for two weeks after that, but then it was eighth grade graduation and summer vacation, so who cared?

High school started a little better. I was still the shortest one in class, but not quite as skinny. Duke still called me The Shrimp, and it still bugged me, but he didn't do it quite as often. I always wanted to slug him, but it didn't seem like the smart thing for me to do.

Sammy seemed to be getting along with him better. That kind of bugged me, but Sammy remained such a good friend of mine, so I had to keep quiet. In sophomore year, they were on the football team together, and in junior year they both made all-state first string. We won our state championship that year.

Again, to the Call

"Sammy, the main reason I called you is I've got some interesting news, and I'd like to go over it with you. I'm not sure how you'll take it, but I wanted to be the first to tell you." I had his attention, finally.

"Sure thing. Am I in some kind of trouble?" Sammy was always in some kind of trouble, but not about this.

"Remember that infamous football practice and what happened to Duke? Remember how it affected both of us?" He couldn't possibly have forgotten, but I had to ask.

"Wow. Yes I remember. I know I wasn't there, but you, along

with the entire school, told me all about it. I know it changed everything for the two of you."

It all went down in the beginning of our senior year. I was the captain of the Debate Team at school, and we were heading into our state competition that weekend. We had a chance to take first place. It would have been a huge boost to our team's membership. We had a big practice planned for right after school in the study hall, but due to some unforeseeable accident with the air conditioner, it felt like 90 degrees in there. It was a nice day outside, so we decided to go out to the stands right by the football field where the team had been practicing.

Duke was our star tight end on the team. He had made first string on the statewide team the past year. Their afternoon practice was over, and all the coaches were gone for the weekend. It was a beautiful, sunny afternoon, 75 degrees outside, no breeze, a great day. Duke and three other players decided to do some passing plays out on the field. One quarterback, three receivers, fantastic weather.

They were running some long pass plays right in front of where we were practicing our debate skills. Duke and the other two guys were running deep routes, cutting left and right, one trying to intercept, and the other two trying to catch. It was actually quite fun to watch. There were six of us in the stands, fielding different questions and answering like we'd do at the state meet. We had an incredibly impressive team and we were deep into the debate when I heard the hollering.

"Hey! Help! We need help! Right now! Help! Help! Now!"

Duke was on the field, laying on his back. For just an instant, I thought about that trick we played on him with the ketchup, but these were seniors, not eighth graders. This was serious. The team and I were over the benches in front of us in seconds. Duke was passed out and turning bluish. I was the only one who knew CPR, good thing for the photographic memory. I worked on Duke while one of the other receivers ran for the phone.

I pumped on his chest, and the two other players took turns breathing into his mouth. They were afraid to pump on him, they figured they'd break his ribs. They were probably right. We worked on Duke for about 15 minutes before the rescue squad came. They rushed him away to the hospital, where he spent four days for observation. He had an episode of 'Sudden Death Syndrome.'

Duke recovered very nicely. He got tons of support from everyone in school, students, teachers, all the custodians and aids. He was elected Prom King, and Nancy, the girl who played one of the nurses, was his Queen.

Duke and Sammy both stopped playing football after that, and there was never another hint of bullying. Our entire school went on an anti-bullying campaign the rest of that year. We also took it to all the schools that fed into our high school.

My size became pretty much a moot point after that.

Our debate team came in third place. We were so shook up by what happened out on the football field that afternoon, we had a hard time concentrating on any of the debate questions and how to answer them. But we all agreed, it was a good thing we went outside to practice that day. Lucky thing for Duke the air conditioner broke down.

The Close

I finally got Sammy's attention, "Sammy, the reason I'm calling you is about what happened after Duke's problem. You know how we got the whole school going on that anti-bullying campaign?"

"Yeah, yeah, yeah. I remember all that. What's that got to do with me?"

Sammy could sometimes get a little self-centered.

"Remember how we got all those other schools involved. Our local Rotary Club and the Chamber of Commerce even got involved with anti-bullying." I was starting to get excited about this.

"Yeah, but I wasn't even around when that all went down. Am I in some kind of trouble now? Is Duke trying to get even with me?"

Just a little self-centered.

"No, no, no, but our United States Senator, you know, Mr. Fredrickson, got wind of all that and he wants Duke and me to be the poster guys for an anti-bullying program."

"He what? You two? No way!" Now I had his attention.

"Yes, and he wants to do those huge billboards with our pictures on them, all along the state highways. He wants to do flyers for every school in the state. Mr. Fredrickson was going on and on and on about his plans." I sure would have liked to see Sammy's face when I said that.

"What? You and Duke on a billboard? You're kidding!"

"No, I'm not kidding, he thinks it could possibly lead to a total country wide program, you know, the whole USA. He wants Duke and me to be a crucial part of it. Duke and me, on billboards, across the whole country. What'd you think about that?" I had him now.

I can still hear my dear friend Sammy, laughing.

WHAT IF – *The air conditioner hadn't broken down?*

Going Solo for the First Time

Today's the day I'm on my own!
Am I brave enough, or am I really a scaredy cat?

In the Beginning

My name is Amy, and I've been preparing for this day for three years. I'm incredibly excited, and I'm scared silly, all at the same time. It's Wednesday, June 8, 2005, at 8:30 in the morning. The sky is a beautiful, light heavenly blue. The temperature makes you want to spend the entire day in your swimsuit, and there's a breeze that couldn't move a feather off your shoulder. In other words, it's a perfect day. A great day for my solo trip.

"Babe, are you just about ready? You've been up since six this morning. Are you saying one last prayer?"

That's what my husband Erik asked me early this morning. He's called me Babe ever since our college days 20 years ago.

"Yeah, I'm all set, but it's not just one last prayer, I'm doing the whole rosary. You know I've been worried about this day for the past six months. Don't you?" I was way more scared than I let on.

"Yeah Babe, I know you've been worried. No matter how many times I tell you not to worry, you just worry, worry, and worry some more. Makes no sense to me."

How could a guy understand?

"That's because you've done this 1,000 times, or more. This is my first solo attempt." I know I shouldn't be worried. I know I'm as ready as I'll ever be. I know all that, but in the back of my mind I also know what can happen. That's what scares me. Scares me plenty.

I've been with Erik on what seems like 1,000 trips, maybe even 2,000. We've been on trips that took two hours and trips that lasted a full week. I've climbed up into that rig of ours so many times I don't even have to look where I'm going anymore. It's second nature to me. I'm generally riding shotgun, as they say, but occasionally, he'll let me take over.

Those are the great trips!

We've been through rainstorms when the rain came down so fast and furious the wipers were almost useless. I'd see them going back and forth and wonder why they were even on. We've been in fog so heavy I could hardly see the front of the rig. I'd think we should stop, but no one else was stopping. Those were white knuckle moments.

Then we've been out on days like this. Days where we could see stunning mountain ranges stretching for miles, lovely blue lakes off in the distance, small town America on the horizon and the skyline of a huge metropolis straight ahead. What wonderful memories we've had, and now I'm about to create my own. I hope.

Today I go solo. I conquer my fear!

The hardest part for me is always getting up into the rig. It's the climb up that gets me. I'm terrified of heights. No kidding, I'm terrified. Once I'm in the rig I'm fine. I've got that shell around me. It's protecting me, and it makes me feel safe. It's just the climb up. It should be so simple.

"Babe, you want some help getting up there? I know you haven't been crazy about heights since you were 7."

That's the last thing I needed to hear.

"No, Eric, I'll be fine. Just let me relax for a minute, or maybe, two." I was actually wishing for a couple of hours.

The Garage

My fear of heights goes back to my brother Todd, and the old apple tree in the backyard. Todd was six years older than I was, and a tad on the mean side, but just a tad. When it happened, I was scrawny and only 7, but he was 13 and a terror. We had this old apple tree in the backyard, next to the garage. One of those majestic ones with branches coming out from every place. It was never trimmed, it made for better climbing. "Just leave the branches grow," that's what Dad always said.

Todd and some of his buddies used to climb up into the old apple tree. Then they'd jump about a foot down right onto the garage roof, and then one by one they'd proceed to jump straight down onto the ground. It was always fun to watch. They created an area about ten feet long, by about six feet wide, and they put about 12 inches of sand on top of it to soften their fall. They'd climb, jump, laugh—climb, jump, laugh—climb, jump, laugh, till it just about drove me crazy. Crazy with envy.

One day Todd said, "Hey, Pipsqueak, why don't you join us up here, or are you a scaredy cat? You like eating apples from our tree, maybe you should learn how to climb up into it."

Not to be outdone, I hollered up to my brother and said, "I'm not a pipsqueak or a scaredy cat. I bet I can climb better than you can. All I need is a lift up to the first branch. I'll show you." That seemed like the right thing to say—at the time.

"Hey, Fred. Will ya give the pipsqueak a lift up to the first branch? She thinks she can do this." Fred was Todd's best friend and I had a crush on him. I was thrilled that he was going to touch me.

"I don't know Todd, she's pretty little." What a great guy, this Fred fella.

"Don't sweat it, Fred. She's pretty good at this kind of stuff, 'sides, what can go wrong? We're here to protect her anyway." I imagined myself in Fred's arms, and him looking down at me with those big blue eyes and smiling.

"Will you guys quit jabbering and get me up to that first branch? I'll show all of you, just get me up there." I was probably getting a little too confident.

Fred gave me a lift up into the tree, and with a little squirming I managed to get up above the roof of the garage. Just one problem. My shoelace got caught on one of the small branches, and I tumbled down onto the garage roof. I landed on my side and rolled about eight feet down toward the edge of the roof, and then, I went right off the roof and into the sand about eight feet below.

"Hey, Fred. Is she dead?" That's what I heard.

"I'm not sure, Todd. Let me check." I was totally embarrassed.

I rolled over, sat up, and started crying. What did they do? They all started laughing. This time it didn't drive me crazy with envy; it just drove me crazy. I ran and hid behind the big concrete container out by the alley, where my dad put all the ashes from our big old coal-fired furnace. The only things that I hurt were my pride and my right big toe. At 7 years old, the only thing that really mattered was my pride, especially living with my big brother.

Come to think about it, maybe the climb up into our rig is

about eight feet, same as the fall off the garage roof. I never thought about that before.

Confidence Builder

"Well Babe, what do you think? You ready for this? I know you can do it. You know you can do it too."

Erik's confidence in me was comforting, but I thought it was a little overrated.

"Easy for you to say, you've done this thousands of times. How many times have you let me take over in the last few years, maybe 100?" I believe Erik was trying to calm me down, I was grateful for that.

"Way, way, way more than that, and you've never goofed up. I know you're ready, you've just got the jitters. It's normal, you ain't scared, you're just nervous. Now get going." He's the love of my life.

"You're probably right. I'm all set—I think." I heard myself say that, but I'm not totally sure I meant it.

"Get up, get into our rig, and have some fun. I'll see you tonight. I'll be waiting for you with a hug, a kiss, and a stiff drink, or two." That was the first thing I heard in an hour and a half that made me smile.

The Rig

Our "rig" is a 1974 Beechcraft Bonanza Aircraft Model 35. Rather than a regular tail, it has the infamous V-Tail, sometimes referred to as 'the scissor tailed doctor killer.' It seats six, but that's crowding it. It's a touchy little plane. I have to keep it well within its limits. It'd be easy for me to lose control if I pushed it too hard. That's why Erik loves it. He's a daredevil. I'm not. He loves to fly it alone, and he named it 'The Hawk.' Let me explain what could happen with the V-Tail Bonanza when pushed too much.

I could be driving a beautiful, mint condition, midnight blue, 1963 split rear window Corvette Stingray. With those beautiful, wide, white racing stripes coming up over the hood, across the top, and down the sleek back end. The number 13 on both doors, 12 inches tall, Times Bold typestyle, and done in 14 karat gold leaf. Everyone in town is giving me the thumbs up and smiling as I slowly drive down Main Street.

The little boys are racing me down to the corner as fast as their clumsy feet will go, laughing and waving all the way. Making bets as to who can beat me to the stop light. Perfect car. Perfect day. Perfect drive. No sweat.

Now imagine I'm in that same Corvette up at the Road America racetrack in Elkhart Lake, Wisconsin. I push it to the limit, get the RPMs up past the red line, and listen to the engine wailing, screaming for me to shift up to the next gear. And out there on turn number three, just before that long straight-away, I very well might do a spin out, go through the hay bales, hit the gravel, and flip over five or six times never to be heard from again. That beautiful, mint condition, 1963 midnight blue Corvette split-window Stingray of mine, would be a hunk of fiberglass and metal, albeit an expensive hunk.

That's the way the V-Tail Bonanza can work. Now, it's all up to me. When we fly as a family, Erik's incredibly cool, no tricks, no nonsense. When he's alone—lookout. "Call me when you're back at the hanger." That's what I tell him when he leaves the house. We've had our plane for just over six years, and we take a lot of trips and family vacations with it. Erik is instrument rated; all he needs to see is the instrument panel. He can fly in any kind of condition.

Rainstorms, blinding fog, whatever Mother Nature throws at him. Not me, I need to see where I'm going.

Now it's my turn to go solo, but I'm scared silly. I can feel the sweat on my forehead and the stickiness on my palms. I think I'm almost ready to pass out.

I met Erik in college, right after he got his solo license. He started flying when he was 16. He heard about this cute chick who was deathly afraid of heights, and he was going to cure me. He was the kind of guy your mother warned you about, your brother was jealous of, and your dad envied. He's mellowed quite a bit since our college days. We have a daughter, Lilly, who's the love of our lives. We're self-employed, and we have a small crew that works for us. We have, of all things, a pawn shop. Erik thinks it's exciting. He named it 'The Sky's the Limit.'

"Amy, I looked over your flight plans, and everything seems to be super organized. A lot more than anything I ever saw Erik do. You shouldn't have any problems, and if, for some reason you do, you can contact me with your radio." That's what my instructor Brad said to me when we got to the airport.

"Thanks Brad, I hope it looks good. I worked on it for two weeks, and Erik thought it was fine." I was pleased with myself for the first time that morning.

"Well, you've got the three airports picked out, and they're all good ones. Looks to me like you should be back here sometime between four and five this afternoon. With any luck." He said that with a smile on his face.

"Brad! What do you mean, WITH ANY LUCK?" He had gotten my attention.

"I'm just kidding, Amy. That's the way pilots talk. You've got to get with the jargon. OK? I've been instructing you for six months, you'll be just fine. I'm completely confident in your ability." Guys have a strange way of talking sometimes.

"Brad, I sure hope so." What else could I say. He couldn't see my sweaty palms or hear my heart racing.

First Leg

I had to plan the four routes I'm flying today. The first three to different airports, and the last one is back to our home base. It was quite a task, but if you're flying solo you've got to know how to plan routes and estimate your time of arrival.

I landed at Cassville, WI, right on the Mississippi River, at 10:15 a.m., right on time. It was a beautiful flight. I came in right over two blue silos on a dairy farm, just before you get to the runway. They look like a double barrel shotgun sticking up out of the ground ready to shoot you down if you goof up. Erik and I have flown here many times for pancake breakfast fly-ins. I've landed twice and taken off three times before, so it turned out to be a piece of cake.

The thing with landing is if you overshoot the runway, after about 200 feet, you'd be down on the bank of the Mississippi river—not fun.

On the other hand, when I take off, it's stunning, I'll climb up over the mighty Mississippi and up over the cliffs on the west side of the river. It's a sight that has to be seen from the air to really be appreciated. My good fortune. All I have to do is make sure the flaps are working. No problem.

"So, are you actually telling me you just flew in from East Troy, and you're working on getting your solo license?" He seemed interested enough.

"Sure thing friend, and so far, so good. My name's Amy, and I just did my first solo leg. One down and three to go." I was pretty proud of myself.

"But, you're a girl. Right?" Strange question.

"Thanks for noticing. I think I am." What else was I supposed to say?

"I noticed your wedding ring, what's your husband think? Is he nuts?" This guy was getting under my skin.

"Well, if you were with him when he stalls this thing at 5,000 feet, you might think so. But I don't. I trust, and love Erik." I thought, Erik could fly circles around you—you hillbilly, you.

"Erik, huh, I'll have to check him out. I'm always looking for a stunt pilot, or a crop duster. Well, best of luck to you." The sooner I got away from this bozo the better.

"Don't need luck, I'm fine. See you up in the sky sometime."

I thought, "phooey on you, I could do your crop dusting as well as anybody." I got in the plane and took off right on time at 10:45 a.m. I stuck my tongue out at my new 'buddy' as I was lifting off.

Huh?

The takeoff from Cassville was magnificent. It went without a hitch, even with sweaty palms. I landed up in Eagle River, WI, right at 12:57 p.m., just 12 minutes behind schedule. I came in right over the golf course and over the tops of those two majestic pines. They were planted there, one right after the other, to get you right in line with the runway. Sure helped me. The first thing I did was get out of the plane and kiss the ground.

It's lovely country up there with all the lakes and the State Forest. Erik and I have flown there quite a few times. Our good friends have a summer cottage on one of the lakes. After landing I had quite a list of things to check over. It's normal maintenance after taking off and landing a couple of times, you know, better safe than sorry.

"So, you're telling me that you just flew in from Cassville? All by yourself. And you're attempting to get your solo license." Oh no, not another bozo.

"Right on, buddy." This fella looked like a real pilot, someone who'd been around a few times. Someone you could trust; he couldn't be a bozo. Could he?

"Wow. Well congratulations. I'm incredibly proud of you. Flying solo takes guts for anyone, guy or gal." What a guy, I knew I'd like him right from the start.

"Thanks! Say, my name is Amy, and in all the excitement this morning, I forgot my cooler with my lemonade and blueberry muffin. Is there a diner around here?" All the nervousness made me thirsty.

"Better than that, I've got an extra ham and cheese on rye and a diet Coke, if you'd like. I thought about going up for a little while this afternoon, I'm going to do some aerobics. I sure am glad I was here when you came in." Nice fella.

"Thanks, I'd love a sandwich and Coke. From here I'm heading over to Green Bay. I've never been there before, but I heard it's supposed to be pretty." I was hoping for some advice.

"Yep, it's gorgeous. Especially coming in from over the water, but it can get tricky with the updraft from the lake." Didn't need to hear that.

"Thanks for the info. I'm supposed to contact them when I'm

up in the air and give them my ETA." Now I was sounding like a real pilot. I was proud of myself once again.

"Yeah, I know, that's part of the solo test. Stop at one airport you've never been to before. Get their OK, give them your coordinates, etc. Shouldn't be any problem for you. Right?"

"Hope not. Well, I've got to get going, I have this schedule I've got to keep up with. You know how it goes." I was getting a little nonchalant, at least that's what I thought.

"Yep, and here's my phone number. I want you to call me when you get back home. Promise? Maybe someday you, Erik, and I can go up together." I was really getting to like this guy, he made me feel like I fit in.

"That would be fun. I promise I'll call when I'm home. Thanks, happy flying to you. Say, what's your name?" I never thought to ask earlier.

"Orville."

"Orville, WOW." That's all I could muster up.

As I was getting ready to leave my new friend Orville, and the Eagle River airport, I couldn't help but notice the name painted on the side of his biplane, 'The Kitty.' I thought, I'm flying 'The Hawk', he's flying 'The Kitty,' his name—no, it was way too much for me to contemplate.

Updrafts & Sideways

I took off from Eagle River, right at 1:45 p.m. Now I was 15 minutes behind schedule, but it didn't seem too bad. The takeoff was a little bumpy. It looked like there were some clouds forming out west, and there was more turbulence than this morning. The Bonanza bounced around a little, but I thought everything was just fine.

At least for the time being.

I contacted the control tower at Green Bay and got all my coordinates and clearances for landing. I figured that things were going swell.

"Amy, this is Frank, over at the traffic control tower at the Green Bay airport. Come in please." Why would he be calling me back?

"This is Amy, what's up Frank?" I wondered if I should be worried.

"Well, there's a front coming in from the west, and we're re-routing you out over Lake Michigan. We want you to use runway number three, and you'll be coming in from over the water. Got that?" Over the water, updrafts, that got me thinking.

"I've got it. How strong is the wind? As I told you this is my solo test, but I have landed into some fairly strong winds, some with gusts up to 30 miles per hour." I exaggerated on the speed; they may have been 20 miles per hour.

"Then this shouldn't be any problem for you. The wind here is no more than 15 miles per hour. Coming in from that direction will make landing a lot easier, and more enjoyable for you. Enjoy the view from up over the water. Don't sweat it." How easy for a guy in the tower to say, that's what I thought.

"Thanks Frank. Got it. Over and out." I'm not worried. I'm not a scaredy cat. I've got this all under control, I hope. That's what I kept telling myself.

I landed at the Green Bay airport at 2:52 p.m., and now I was 22 minutes behind schedule, oh well. I did have to come in a little sideways because of the "breeze," as they called it, but I got it straightened out at the correct spot and came in fine. I was actually quite proud of myself, but Frank just said, "nice landing kid."

I found a small café at the airport and had some coffee and relaxed for half an hour, while I tried to get my nerves back in shape. The Diet Coke and sandwich over in Eagle River didn't settle to well, and for the last half hour all I wanted to do was get up, walk to the back of the plane, and use the lavatory. I couldn't do that very well in our little Bonanza, so I tried crossing my legs. One more take-off and one more landing and I'll have that stiff drink and get my solo license.

"Honey, you look frazzled. What's up? You want another cup-a-joe?" If it wasn't for my bladder I'd have asked for a gallon.

"Well, your nametag reads Linda, so, Linda, I'm working on getting my solo license. This last landing was a little bit tricky and I have one more leg to go. I should be home by 4 or so, I'm not super worried, but I am a little stressed out. And now to top it all off, I hear there's a front coming in from the west." You can tell a stranger something you may not tell a friend.

"WOW. Hats off to you. I applaud you. Listen, that storm isn't due here till well after midnight. You said you were going to be home by four or so, now don't sweat it. Go girl go, you can do it." Maybe that was just the confidence builder I needed.

I felt much better after that little exchange, and all I needed to do was one more leg of the trip. How tough could that be? I got in the Hawk and took off at exactly 3:30 p.m., just 30 minutes behind schedule. Brad had told me not to get too worked up about the times. He said, "Remember, even the major airlines fall behind sometimes. It's just part of the business." Now I understand.

The Co-Pilot
Bumpety, Bumpety, Bumpety, Bumpety, Bump. That's how tough it could be.

There were plenty of clouds forming out to the west, but they did stay near the Mississippi River. I only encountered three massive clouds where I was able to bank down between two of them, and then up and over the third. I was pretty pleased with myself, until I caught a small downdraft and bit my lip a couple of times. I thought about that 1963 Corvette Stingray flipping over, and I settled down.

I got back to East Troy at exactly 4:38 p.m., just 38 minutes past four; however, it was 22 minutes before five. Brad was thrilled with my performance, Erik acted nonchalant, but I think he was overwhelmed. I had remained much calmer than I would have expected. I think some of it had to do with the fact that I did have an 8 x 10 glossy photo of Erik propped up in the co-pilot seat all day. Just for moral support!

Three weeks later I received my solo pilot's license. Erik and I had a celebratory week-long vacation up north in Eagle River. We got well acquainted with Orville and his plane.

WHAT IF – Amy hadn't fallen off that garage roof and been afraid of heights?

First Mate to the Rescue

NOAH BUILT THE ARK!

That's what the sign with the changeable letters out in front of our church said on that beautiful spring Sunday morning back in 1959. I was walking right next to Dad that morning. I noticed him stop and do a double take when he read it.

"Chuck, do you see that sign about Noah and the Ark?" I think Dad scratched his head when he asked me that.

I thought that was an odd question considering I was right next to Dad, but it was Sunday morning and we were at Church, so I played along. "Sure do, Dad. Why are you so interested in it anyway? I noticed you scratch your head, what gives?" He seemed puzzled.

"I'm not sure, it just took me off guard. You know all about my love for boats, but Noah and the Ark, what's with that? Is that some kind of strange message?" I was beginning to wonder about dear old Dad.

"Whatever." What else was I supposed to say? We weren't even supposed to be at our church today. Mom, Dad, and the rest of the family were supposed to be in Chicago visiting Dad's buddy Larry. I was going to be with Tammy at the races all day. If Dad hadn't forgot to replace the battery in his car, I'd be 50 miles away. Now I'm stuck here.

"What do you mean, whatever? You sure don't sound very sympathetic. You're a kid, you're supposed to have all the answers." He's never said that to me before.

Dad could get a little testy sometimes, especially about boats. I always chalked it up to his years in the Navy during the war. He served most of his time aboard an aircraft carrier that all the guys called 'The Ark.' He's had some fascinating stories about the fellows from those days, just nothing much about the war.

"OK, Dad. Now let's get into church before they start without us."

I still don't remember anything about the sermon from that day. I just remember it was a gorgeous day, and I wanted to be up at the races. I was 19, had a wonderful girlfriend named Tammy, and a cool chopped and channeled '49 Merc. The original 'Lead Sled,' all in satin black.

Mom was with us, along with my younger brother and two little sisters. We left church to go have breakfast with Dad's brother Elmer and his family. It was just a two-block walk. No big deal. Just me and the family, lucky me.

WHAT HAVE YOU DONE!

That's what the sign said when we left church. Someone had changed the copy during Mass. Dad not only stopped and did a double take, this time he did scratch his head, and he scribbled down both sayings on the back of the church bulletin.

"Chuck, do you see that sign? What the heck's going on? Who changed the copy? I talked with Lee, our head usher, he thought that message was on there all week. Now it's different. Am I seeing things?"

"You're not seeing things. I see the same sign. Somebody must be messing with you. Why do you care about Noah and the Ark? Just chalk it up to coincidence." By that time, I just wanted to get home.

For some reason, it seemed like a lot for Dad to take in. He appeared puzzled. Why? We weren't supposed to be at our church that day. They were all supposed to be in Chicago visiting his buddy Larry. Dad met Larry in the Navy during the war. Dad, feeling it was his patriotic duty, and his hatred for Hitler, joined in January 1942 and was released in the fall of 1945. Larry joined the day after Pearl Harbor and retired from the Navy as a Naval Captain. Dad met Larry on the USS Enterprise, he always said it was one of the luckiest things that ever happened to him. I believe Larry saved Dad's life one day, but neither would ever talk about it.

After the Navy, I know Dad never lost his love of the water and boats, but why was he so intrigued about Noah and the Ark?

By 1959, our family had grown. Of the four kids, I was the oldest. My brother was 13, little sis was 9 and baby sis was 6. Was Dad starting to think about having his own boat, or did he think it was too late? Was that the message? 'Noah built the ark'— 'What have you done?' It seemed to intrigue Dad. Was it telling him something? Was it really a message just for him, or was it just a coincidence? We'd find out a few years later.

That same summer my Uncle Al rented a cottage on an incredibly beautiful lake. It was just an hour's drive north to get there, and the last five miles went right through one of our pristine state forests. It was a beautiful drive, winding road through tall regal pine trees, crossing over three small creeks. What a summer that was. What memories we created. There were five families enjoying the lake and all the activities, water skiing, sail boating, swimming, fishing, anything to do with water and fun. Times were good, but Dad remained puzzled.

"Chuck, I'm still perplexed by that sign at church last spring.

How'd you like to go with me to the boat show downtown tomorrow? I think it might be kind of fun, just you and me."

I wondered about Mom.

"Sure, sounds like fun to me." How could a 19-year-old guy pass that up?

"Let's not tell your Mother about it yet. We can just go down and look at things." Dad sometimes had a sneaky side to him, I always figured it came from bunking with 200 other guys on The Enterprise.

"I think we'd better tell Mom. I know she doesn't like secrets or surprises, at least not that kind. I don't want to get in trouble. I'm not worried about you." Secretly I was a little worried, but it was more about his confusion.

"I'll tell her when we get home. She wouldn't want to go anyway. She's not that crazy about boats."

I think that had something to do with Dad's time in the Navy.

Well, Dad and I went to the 1960 boat show downtown, just to look. I believe the message about; 'What have you done,' the rented summer cottage up at the lake, and the time in the Navy, was getting to Dad. His love of the water and boats seemed to be festering. Was Dad getting impatient? Was he thinking about getting his own 'Ark'?

The 50s and 60s were times of great prosperity in the USA. There were new car designs every year. New houses in new subdivisions, rock 'n roll, Elvis, and jobs galore. The country was booming. However, Dad came of age during the Great Depression, so he knew tough times. He knew what it was like to not have enough, to not have a chicken in every pot.

Sometimes, when he'd get a little melancholy, he'd tell us how he used to go around with his little red coaster wagon, looking for pieces of wood. It was during the great depression, and it was to help his Dad heat the house. Or how he remembered his Mom and Dad having those talks around the kitchen table about possibly losing the house.

He talked about the times all the relatives would get together on Sunday afternoons with all the kids at the city park and sing songs. They'd put all the food together and have a picnic, all in the hopes of raising everybody's spirits. The Depression was tough. Now, Dad seemed to be wondering if he was stuck in that way of thinking, and possibly not adjusting to the new prosperity. It seemed to be a tough time for Dad.

The Plan

Dad and I went back to the boat show in January of 1961. This time with Mom's blessing of course. Boy, was he getting the bug. The summers of 1959 and 1960, up at the lake, that's what the entire family was calling Uncle Al's cottage. Those were great summers. They must have planted the bug in him, and it just started festering. It wouldn't go away, it kept gnawing away at him. Poor Dad.

"Chuck, good grief, look at some of these boats? I've never seen anything like it. Things sure have changed since my Navy days." Said Dad, excitedly.

"Yep, they sure are beauties, but look at some of the prices." I spent most of the day with my mouth half open in amazement.

"Boy, would I like to get Larry up here to see some of these babies, I think he'd be amazed. Back in the Navy everything was one color, and it was drab over drab. These are incredible." I could tell Dad was getting excited, and I wanted to bring him back to reality. I thought I'd try the money thing, it always worked when he tried it on me.

"Yeah, but some of these cost more than you and Mom paid for our house. I do like that wood Chris-Craft Capri over in the corner though. What do you think about that beauty?" Now I was getting excited, even though I was darn near broke.

"I think it's fantastic, but on your apprentice pay you'd need to work all three shifts. That just doesn't sound like you, and you'd never see Tammy." Dad always was the sensible one, and it seemed the money issue was hitting home.

Dad came home from the boat show a little deflated, but just a little. The 1961 show was a doozy. Boats came in every imaginable shape, just like the new cars. There were colors with names I'd never heard of before, and shades I couldn't imagine. And the names, holy cow, they made you want to write a check on the spot. Good planning and marketing by the boat companies.

In the 1960s, a good machinist made darn good money, and that's what Dad became after the Navy. Dad worked his way up to become the head foreman of a major manufacturing company in the Midwest and was near the top of his pay scale. He still had three kids in private schools, and that cost darn good money also. The prices for the new boats at the show in 1961 were steep for a guy with four kids, a mortgage, and the private school thing. Dad never would have pulled my brother and sisters out of the private school just to buy a boat. Therein lay the one obstacle that Dad had to overcome.

So…being an incredibly smart guy, Dad hatched a plan…

"Honey, you know Chuck and I went to the boat show downtown for the past two years. Right?" Dad looked like a 2-year-old caught with his hand in the candy jar.

"Yes, I do." Mom had the look my old high school principal would get.

"You know my time in the Navy kind of got me hooked on boats. Right?"

Go for it Dad.

"Yes, I certainly know that." Mom's jaw looked clenched.

"You know Chuck is already at the age where he may not want to do much with us as a family anymore, and you also know the other kids will feel the same way soon. Right?"

Dad went right for the guilt trip idea.

"Yes, yes, yes, I know all that. But I also know the cost of a boat is pretty darn high, at least according to Chuck. Right?"

Keep me outa this, that's what I was thinking.

"Yeah, that's what Chuck said." I was feeling a little sorry for Dad at that point.

"I also know our kids still have a number of years in the private school system, and that costs an arm and a leg. Right?" Mom was pretty good with the money thing also.

"Well, it's not cheap." Dad may have been on the ropes.

"And, we still have 15 years left on the mortgage. I just don't know how we could afford another payment."

Mom always had a knack about her, she'd get to the chase, no screwing around. Not Mom.

"Yeah, I agree with you, but that's the great part about my plan! I think I could build a boat. I've seen enough of them at the shows, and I think with help from the family, we could do it. The only costs would be the materials and we can spread that out over a couple years. I don't think we'd have to borrow anything."

Dad saved the best for last. Hurray for dear old Dad.

NOAH BUILT THE ARK! WHAT HAVE YOU DONE?

There must have been a message on that sign in 1959. Dad admitted that he never really understood the message, or if it was even for him. If it was, why him? But he also never forgot it. By the fall of 1961, Dad had reviewed more than a dozen various boat plans. He knew he could build a boat with our help. It might not be quite as fancy as some that were at the show, but it'd be paid for, and it'd be a family adventure.

Dad chose a design called 'The First Mate.' It was a wonderful looking boat, 19-feet, 6-inches long by 7-feet, 6-inches wide. It had a neat looking cabin with a windshield and an enclosed front end with storage underneath. The side rails were almost 8 inches wide. It was an extremely stable boat. One person could stand on a side rail with no effect on the boat. Mechanic Illustrated gave it a two thumbs-up and a fist pump in their April 1961, magazine.

At 12:01 a.m. on New Year's Day in 1962, Dad made his first cut into a 2-inch by 8-inch piece of clear pine. It would become part of the main beam. Dad cut for five minutes, the sawdust was flying, and we were all cheering. Then the six of us joined the rest of the relatives, and we all toasted to 'The First Mate.'

We all worked on the boat like there was no tomorrow. Dad was the foreman, and Mom was the chief cook, I was the first mate, and my brother and little sisters were the gofers and helpers. What a team Dad had, brings a chill to me even now, 56 years later. "Measure twice, cut once," "There's a place for everything and everything in its place." Boy, do I remember hearing those suggestions, or were they commandments?

It was a slow process, even with all of us working. We had to cut and assemble all the cross beams, side supports, the main

68

beam, and pieces I don't even remember the names of.

"Chuck, did you set all the screws in the first layer of plywood?"

If Dad would have looked at my hands he never would have asked. I had calluses on my calluses.

"Yeah, Dad I sure did, but I'm not sure I can do anymore for a few days. My hands need a rest." We had to put two layers of 3/8-inch-thick marine grade plywood, soaked down with water, one layer at a time, in order to make the shape of the curved bottom and sides. Then what seemed to me like thousands of wood screws.

"OK, I'll do the second layer. When I'm done, we've got some painting to do. I'd like to get this ready by June." Dad was ever the optimist.

When Dad finished the second layer, we covered the entire bottom and sides with fiberglass. Dad sprayed the paint on, a nice light blue paint for the bottom and sides. When we finally got it turned over, it started looking like a real boat. We went onto the top deck, the flooring, the cabin area, the windshield, the seats, the transom, and on and on. More cutting, sanding, painting, staining, carpeting, and who can remember it all.

We worked on the boat for a little over two years. It turned out beautiful. It sat high on the water. I think it was an extremely proud boat. I know we were proud!

The Verdict

"Well, Honey, what do you think?" Dad asked mom, with a smile a mile wide.

"I think it's great. I'm so proud of you and the kids. I had my doubts when you first mentioned you wanted to build a boat, but

I should have known better." Now Mom looked like a 16-year-old girl who just had her first kiss.

"I'm proud of you also. I never could have done this without your support, and the kids were a fantastic bonus. Plus, the money wasn't too bad."

That was Dad's subtle way of getting off the hook for the money he spent on the motor and the trailer. It worked.

"You know me, I always worry about the money, but you pulled this off. I love you and the boat." Dad's smile just got wider!

"Dad, I'm impressed. Even I had my doubts. You know, it sure would look good behind my '49 Merc. All I'd need is a trailer hitch." I could be subtle too.

"Nice try Chuck, but no thanks, I'll do all the towing of this baby. Besides you and Tammy are getting married next June." I thought, maybe Dad will give the boat to his grandkids.

In the early summer of 1964, Dad launched the boat up at the lake. All the relatives whistled and cheered. He was proud of his family, and we were proud of him. I can still see his smile. We did lots of waterskiing, pulling tubes with kids on them, fishing, and swimming. That summer we took it out on Lake Michigan to watch the Fourth of July fireworks. It seemed like we were in a flotilla of boats and Dad was thrilled. It reminded him of his Navy days, back when he was aboard 'The Ark.' It was an incredibly exciting time for all of us, even with what happened next.

Bump & Flip

It happened on a sunny, calm, Saturday morning in late July. My good friend Tom and I decided to do some fishing up at the lake. We got there around seven in the morning. We didn't have much sleep the night before, so we were running at half-speed. It took about 30 minutes to get everything loaded, and we were off for a good day of fishing.

The lake had some neat shoreline features. There were four streams that came into it, one nice-sized creek that flowed out of it, and a channel that connected to a small pond. The channel was too small for our boat, but we could easily canoe up into the pond. It was a popular area for the Boy Scouts. They came from as far as 75 miles just to earn their merit badges for canoeing.

The area around the channel always attracted the biggest fish, so we headed up there. It was up on the north end of the lake. To this day, I'll never understand why we were the only boat out that morning.

We spotted some Boy Scouts taking off from the opposite shore, in canoes, heading over to the channel. It was just about eight in the morning. There were six canoes, each with three scouts. Great day to earn their merit badges.

At about the halfway point across the lake, two of the canoes bumped into each other. The scouts were acting a little goofy, and not paying attention to each other, not so unusual for young boys. In a canoe, it doesn't take much to flip, and that's just what they did, in about 50 feet of water. The Boy Scouts in the four other canoes were helpless, they were shouting, hollering and close to panicking. Six boy scouts were flailing around in the water, just trying to save themselves.

Tom and I were only about 50 yards away, so it took just a few seconds to get to them. I was able to lean right over the side of our boat and pull all six of the scouts up and out of the water. There were some mighty happy faces in that group. Four of the scouts said they thought they were goners.

All in all, it was a pretty intense period of about five minutes.

Tom and I received honorary life saving merit badges at their next meeting. Dad was the guest of honor at their annual dinner meeting, and he received an honorary Eagle Scout badge, plus a handsome plaque for the construction of the boat. I've never, before or after, seen a man so proud, so happy, so at peace with the world as Dad was that day.

The Boy Scout troop bought an American flag and a Boy Scout flag and rigged up flag holders on the back of the boat, so every other scout troop would recognize it. They had three gold leaf decals made for the boat that said, 'The First Mate.'

'The First Mate' was on the lake until Dad retired in1983. By then it had run its course. Tammy and I made a small area in our backyard with sand and planters that looked like a beach. We put the boat on 'our beach' and it's still being used by our grandkids and neighborhood kids who play 'Pirates of the Caribbean' in it.

Mom and dear old Dad bought a 26-foot RV and are traveling the country 'till the cows come home.'

WHAT IF – Dad had replaced the battery in his car back in 1959, and we hadn't seen the sign?

Jack's Metal Sliver

"Henry, make mine a double, and make it quick!" I was in no mood to be standing around the bar waiting for a lousy little drink.

Ouch

"Damn shame about that last game Jack. Looked like you were having some trouble. What the heck was going on? I thought you guys were a cinch to take first place. What happened?"

I noticed a smirk on Henry's face when he said that.

"Yeah, Henry, I sure was having trouble, serious trouble. Don't remind me about how good my team was supposed to be. I guess some things just aren't meant to be. Now, can I get that drink?" I could've made three drinks while he was babbling.

"Sure, thing Jack. This one's on the house."

No kidding, I thought my whole team deserved one on the house.

Trouble? He thinks I was having trouble. No kidding. It wasn't just trouble; it was a damn nightmare. I don't mind losing, but I can't stand letting my team down. All I needed to bowl was a lousy 150 game. What did I bowl? A crappy 126. Now we're the second-place losers for the rest of the year. It's going to be tough to make up for this fiasco. I'm not sure it's even possible. What a final game. What a last night. I'll just sit here and cry in my drink.

"Yo, Jack, those dudes at the other end of the bar, you know, the jokers that took first place, the Pin Droppers. They love you;

they think you're the greatest. They want to buy your drink— or should I tell them to get lost and just start a tab for you and your team?" Said Henry with a growing smirk.

"Hell, Henry, that's the least they can do. They ought to love me, and they owe me a lot more than a drink. Tell them they'll have to buy my whole team a drink. After that I'll start a tab for my team, if they'll even let me." I was disgusted with myself.

Why did I ever change the oil in that old '58 Chevy wagon? Why didn't I tell my friend Todd to wait till tomorrow? I had plenty of time. Why am I always in such a hurry? What's the big rush? Why didn't I use a shop rag to check the drain plug for leaks, instead of my thumb? Why did I get that stupid metal sliver?

I never even felt the darn thing until the third game, but by then it was next to impossible to get my swollen thumb in the stupid ball. I had to palm the dumb ball, no control, no strikes, and just three spares—pretty pathetic. If only I would have known what a mess it was going to be. So why do I keep tormenting myself? Why do I always have to be the hero?

The Price

"Yo, Jack, Bob and his whole team said they'll gladly buy your team a drink and pay for three extra-large pizzas with all the trimmings plus garlic bread. All you need to do is have your mugshot taken with your nifty little second place trophy." Now Bob was rubbing it in.

"Yeah, sure. I'll do that if they make it quick." That was the least I could do for my team.

"Yeah, but they want you to stand with them and their fantastic, 18-inch tall first place trophy. That silver one with the bowler on top, and those neat chrome columns with the fancy shiny blue foil on the front. The one that says, First Place—Corky's Bowl, 1990." Now Henry was getting on my nerves.

"You tell Bob, he's starting to push it. Tell him I might change my mind any second now, even with those free pizzas." I liked Bob enough, but the whole night was getting out of control.

"Jack, you know I'm just quoting Bob. Hell, Jack, I'm just the bartender. I'd never rub it in that way."

Sure! Henry would never rub it in. Hell, he's Bob's brother-in-law, what else could I expect from him. He's been bugging me and the team all year. That night I almost rolled the 300 game, I swear he doubled up my drink in the seventh frame. Then, I had that dreaded seven-ten split in the tenth frame. Sure, Henry, you'd never rub it in, yeah, and I've got stock in a Portuguese mining company I'd like to sell you.

"Henry, tell Bob it's a deal, but tell him not to rub it in. Tell him I haven't had so much fun since I was in the rice fields in Vietnam. See if that shuts Bob up for a while." I was probably feeling the effects from that first drink.

Vietnam, now that was a hell of a surprise. It was never on my bucket list of places to go to. I didn't even know where the hell it was back then. The idea of traveling halfway around the globe just to get shot at. No thank you. And all for what? Just to get spit at and ridiculed when I got back home by those Commie loving college bums. I knew there were some good college guys around, some of my best friends were off to college, but they never greeted me at the airport when I came home that way. Those were some dark times—really dark times.

It's no wonder I can't get some of those old memories out of my mind. They pop up when I least expect them to, usually when I'm kind of down in the dumps. I remember one of my good buddies over there saying, "shit happens." He said it right after he was shot in the leg. His leg turned out OK, but I never did think that kind of stuff just happens. I think it's all man-made. I know that damn war was certainly man made.

I thought I heard Bob talking. "Hey, Jack, we're ready if you are. Make sure you bring that nifty little 8-inch-tall black bowling pin that says Second Place Losers."

"OK, Bob, but you better make this fast, and you better make this as easy as possible." He was starting to get under my skin, and I could feel my face getting warm.

"Yeah, yeah, yeah, now stand right here in the center of our team. Put on a nice big smile and hold that cute little second place trophy up nice and high. Isn't this going to be fun? What a great picture. Aren't you thrilled?"

That was about the last thing I felt.

Geeze, that lousy metal sliver really messed things up tonight. We were supposed to take first place; it was going to be a cinch. I could roll a 150 game with my left hand, but no, that would be against the rules. Who made that rule? Probably some guy who never bowled. Oh, hell, who cares. Crap, what a night.

"OK, Bob, but now I'm getting mighty thirsty. You know with my size it takes a lot of liquid to quench my thirst. Can we get this over with?" I was done for.

The Old Days

"Yeah, yeah, yeah, I've been hearing about your size ever since the sixth grade. No one ever lets me forget about that day, but I was one of the good guys. Right? You may be bigger than me, but I am faster than you." Bob was fast that day, I think he was scared as hell.

Geez, is Bob ever going to let me forget about that day? It happened a long time ago, but I must have really impressed him. Chalk one up for me. He and three of his buddies from the sixth grade were trying to steal that little kid's bike. I was in fifth grade, but I was a whole lot bigger than any of them. Was I supposed to just let them take it? There were only four of them, and the little kid was really crying. I had to help him; it was second nature for me. Who wouldn't help a crying little kid?

Thinking back, I sure didn't do any thinking. I just started swinging. Two of them wound up on the ground and two of them started running away as fast as they could go. The little kid stopped crying and started smiling. Then he hugged me.

Memories, good old memories. Bob was one of the runners. I didn't find out till two weeks later that Bob was trying to help the kid. He tried to get the bike from his buddies to give it back to the kid. He never really wanted to take it. Good old Bob. We became friends later that year.

"Bob, I know you're older than me, but I can still pick you up by your ankles and shake the change out of your pockets. I've done it once, and I could do it again. And whatever you do, don't send that picture to my brothers and sisters, or you will be hanging by your ankles again!" It was time to get over by my team, if they'd let me.

"Yeah, yeah, yeah, but your problem is you'd have to catch me first. Remember, I'm a lot faster than you. You couldn't catch me in the sixth grade, and you'd never catch me now. Besides, even if you did catch me, your thumb is so darn sore you'd never be able to hold onto me."

Bob had a point. I guess every once in a while a fellow has to be put in his place. Maybe that's what tonight is all about. Maybe I've got to learn something from this whole fiasco. Maybe the sliver was a blessing. Who knows?

"Yo, Jack, would you tell your team to order their pizzas and drinks. The place is emptying out, and I'm running out of things to do back here. Besides, we only make pizzas until 11:30, and its already quarter too." Henry never did much of anything anyway, why should tonight be different?

"Thanks, Henry. Why don't you go talk to Ted? He's over at the corner table with the rest of the team?" About time Henry earns his tips, that's what I thought.

The Team

I absolutely hate letting my team down. If I lose, I can live with it, but letting the team down is another story. I think it started when I was a kid playing baseball and football. The other guys always expected me to save the game. Get a home run here or a touchdown there, but always make the winning score. I tried my best to never let them down. Maybe it's becoming too much for me. I don't know. All I know is I'm tired, I'm thirsty, and my thumb hurts like hell.

It was different with my family. Being right in the middle of seven kids, I could pretty much disappear. I could do what I wanted to do and go wherever I wanted to go. No one in the family ever seemed to miss me. They were always dealing with someone older or someone younger. With three older brothers and three little sisters I think they sometimes wondered, Jack who? Those were the good old days. I really do miss them, there was no pressure, no stress.

The team idea really grew strong over in Vietnam. Over there you had to be part of the team. Everybody's life depended on it. One slip and you had no idea what might happen. It could be the end. I try not to think about those days very often. It makes sleeping tough. Then I heard my co-captain Ted. He's always trying to keep me on the level.

"Hey, Jack, we've got the drinks and three pizzas over here. Are you going to join us for a quick prayer, or sit over there all-night drinking and feeling sorry for yourself?" I picked up on the feeling sorry for myself part.

"Ted, I'm not feeling sorry for myself, and I'm on the way over. I was just thinking about Bob and the bike episode. Save me some pizza and get me another drink."

I was thinking about more than just Bob and the bike episode. I was thinking how there's nothing like having good friends. Friends you've known for over 20 years. Friends you grew up with. Friends you can count on even if they razz you once in a while, even Bob. It makes getting over those memories of rice fields, jungles, and that weird orange stuff they sprayed on the foliage somewhat easier. But, just somewhat.

Growing up in this comfortable little town with farmland all around, and with three gorgeous lakes all within a quarter-mile walk, made the transition to the other side of the globe pretty daunting. Most of us were in the same predicament though. Some guys adjusted fine, and some guys never did. But it's over. I'm back home. I'm putting those memories behind me, at least for now.

"Yo, Jack, I started your tab. Anything else you want?" I was ready for a dose of Advil.

"Thanks, Henry, just set up another round for my team, and

keep the tab open till we leave. I'll square up with you then. Did your brother-in-law Bob pay for the pizzas? Or did he try to squirm his way out of here?" At least Bob and Jack weren't actual brothers.

"Jack, you know me better than that. I can't help who my sister married. So, she picked a jerk. I had nothing to do with that night. I've been supporting your team all year."

I never really understood what happened back on that night. "Uhm, Henry, what about that night—you know the night with the double mixed drink."

"Damn, Jack, the night you missed that 300 game I didn't even mix your drinks. I've been trying to tell you that all year. You just don't want to believe me. You know Charlie was helping me that night. Quit being so darn hard on me, and yourself." There was no smirk on Henry's face right then.

Henry was probably right. That's always been my problem, too hard on myself. I've got to work on that. Boy, my team can really drink. Must be the frustration of coming in second place and getting that stupid little black bowling pin. Maybe it would have been better to come in last place. They got a cute little hula girl bobble head doll that said, 'Also Ran.' There's probably going to be seven little black bowling pins in the trash tomorrow. I really let my team down, and now I feel miserable. Why do I always have to be the hero? Then I heard Bob pipe in.

"Well Jack, I'm really looking forward to next year. Hopefully, you'll make it even closer, if that's possible. This year we took you guys by 25 pins. Maybe next year we can tie and have a marathon roll-off. Wouldn't that be fun. See you later." I thought Bob had left an hour ago.

"Bob, you'd better get your running shoes on or you'll be swinging by your ankles in about three minutes. Right now, that stupid trophy of yours looks a lot taller and smarter than you."

Then I heard Ted chime in, "Jack, you'd better get over here before the pizzas are all gone. And now you've got two drinks waiting for you." Make it a double dose of Advil.

"Ted, I'm heading to the latrine. I'll be over there in a couple minutes. Let's get a picture of our team with our stupid little trophies, before we all toss them in the trash." That's exactly how I was feeling at that moment.

"Stupid little trophy? Toss them in the trash? Toss them like heck. We're all proud of them. Do you have any idea how bad a year it would have been if you weren't our captain and anchor bowler? We might have gotten that dumb little last place bobble head doll. Next year we're going to take first place. We'll bounce Bob and the Pin Droppers right off the alleys. We're a team, and don't you forget it!"

"It's nice of you to say that, Ted, but when I needed to come through for the team, I bowled a lousy 126, and we lost by 25 pins. Now we're the losers for a year. Sorry." I needed a triple dose of Advil.

"Losers! Sorry! What's that all about? Jack, do you have any idea how many times you pulled us through as a team? Remember that night when you opened with two spares and went on to finish with all strikes, and you rolled a 276? We won that night by 16 pins. The entire place was watching and cheering, even Bob and the Pin Droppers. Don't give us any of that sorry crap, and we're not losers. We're a team, and we're winners, thanks to you."

The Re-Cap

Well that's pretty much how it all happened.

We were all sitting around the bar at Corky's Bowl, after the last game of the season, that night back in 1990. My name is Ted, and I'm proud to say I was Jack's co-captain back then. We lost Jack on September 10, 2007, just four days before his 62nd birthday. The official report was 'complications from pneumonia,' but we all figured it was Vietnam and that Agent Orange stuff.

No one ever wanted to talk about that stuff, but Jack told us what it did to all the landscape. He told us how the military called it Operation Ranch Hand, but how the soldiers would sit around and say, "Only you can prevent a forest," and they'd talk about how Smokey the Bear would have to retire. He always thought it was ironic that he was from such a green part of the country. So many trees, lakes, fields, and forests. Over there was similar, till Operation Ranch Hand. He didn't like that, that was his personal opinion. That was that.

He never planned on going to Vietnam, not many did. His number came up first when they did the lottery based on birthdays. He figured it'd be better for him if he joined rather than being drafted. It was a good decision on his part. Once he was in the Marines, he was total USA. Jack was always a great team player, and you could always count on him.

I remember the day four of us were on a golf course on the east coast. It was in 1991, right after Operation Desert Storm. A squadron of military planes flew over us rather low and in formation, Jack figured they were returning from Iraq. Three of us stood there and waved and kind of saluted. Jack stood there at attention, with tears streaming down his face. He loved his team, any team, and his teams loved him.

We always wondered though, about that metal sliver he picked up from that '58 Chevy. We all kind of thought it was a blessing. It made Jack more human, more like the rest of us.

Jack carried us. Six of us carried Jack, three on each side.

Isn't that what friends are for?

WHAT IF – Jack had used a rag to check the oil in that '58 Chev, rather than his thumb?

Jack's Pledge to His Team

25 years can be a lifetime, and a lifetime can go by in a flash!

The Questions

"So, Bud, you think you've got it tough. Really, or is it always just about you? What about the rest of us? Do we still matter to you as a team?"

That's how my conversation with Bud started three days ago at his 70th birthday party. All because of the pledge our bowling team made 25 years ago, at Corky's Bowl, back in 1990. We lost first place to the Pin Droppers, but we still had our pride. Jack, our captain, thought we were losers because of him. We did our best trying to convince him that we were thrilled with the year, the team, and him. But Jack never liked losing, he wanted us to be winners, so he had a plan, all we had to do was finish it. It was on our shoulders now.

"Yeah, Ted, I think I've had it pretty darn tough. You know I had both hips replaced in the last two years. You know I've been through some tough rehab. My doc says to be careful; he doesn't like the idea of my straining them. What do you want from me anyway?" Bud, the constant whiner.

"I want you to get enthused again. The whole team made that pledge, we all agreed with Jack. Matter of fact, we were all pretty darn excited about it. We didn't know what 25 years would bring."

Bud never was the most optimistic fellow, he had kind of a life sucks attitude sometimes. Oh well, that's Bud.

"Well Ted, I think Jack was drunk. I said it then, and I'm saying it now. Besides, who were we to disagree? He carried us the whole year, and we couldn't even bowl good enough to cover his lousy 126 game."

Bud had a good point, we were so used to Jack saving the day, maybe we just took it for granted that he'd do it again that night. "Bud, you know he never blamed us." I tried to remind Bud.

"Well, I still think we were a bunch of schmucks. We thought he'd carry us as usual. We were all willing to just go along for the ride that night." Maybe Bud was, but not me.

"Well, Bud, you can think what you will, but we all agreed with Jack that night. Now the 25 years is up. Happy birthday and forget about your hips and think about your team for once." I hadn't seen Bud in a few months and was hoping for a more positive response. I figured maybe he just needed more prodding.

"Ted, if you remember, which you never like to do unless it suites your fancy, Johnnie wouldn't take the pledge that night. Go bug him!"

I was getting a little ticked with Bud.

"Bud, what the hell's wrong with you? We were all in our 40s, and Johnnie was 64. He was our substitute bowler, and he sponsored our team. He's 89 now, you do know that, don't you?" I wondered if Bud's brain went out with his hips.

"OK, Ted, just to keep you quiet, I'll be there. I'll do it for Jack's memory. You win, now just leave me alone." That wasn't a problem.

Bud used to be a lot more fun. There was that New Year's Eve party when he danced to "Macho-Macho-Man" with the lampshade on his head. Or the year he shot two deer from his tree stand on opening morning, within four minutes of each other. He was back at deer camp with two dressed-out deer hanging on the deer rack before some of us even got out of bed. I guess 25 years can take a toll on a guy. Those damn hips.

Dave and Matt were also on the team. It was Jack, Bud, Matt, Dave, and me—quite the team. They both liked the pledge idea, but that was 25 years ago. We've talked about it a lot since then, but now push comes to shove. We bowled together as a team until 2008. The last seven years have been hard on all of us, all except Jack, he's gone on to his final reward. I'm sure he has a huge trophy case up there just for him, no losers up there, not around Jack.

I was kind of nervous about approaching Dave after my discussion with Bud. "Dave, remember that pledge we made with Jack back in 1990, right after our last game at Corky's place? You were incredibly excited about it that night. Are you still excited, or have you fizzled out?" I was cautious.

"Heck yeah, Ted. I remember, I've been waiting 25 years for this. I haven't mentioned it often because I know how Bud feels. I know how easy it is to tick Bud off. Then he gets all upset and says things he regrets. It just isn't worth it." Dave sure knows Bud.

"Well, I just had that conversation with Bud, and you're right. He's not excited about the pledge, he blames his hips. I did remind him about the team, I think he might come around. I sure hope so." I was trying to keep Dave pumped up.

"Yeah, Ted. Bud never was the gutsy type. He'd dance around with that stupid lampshade on his head, but he wouldn't go up with us in that hot air balloon last summer. I always thought he was kind of a wimp. Maybe I should have a talk with him."

The two of them never got along, kind of like water and oil. "Dave, I think you should leave him alone until Saturday. Once he has a couple beers, he should be fine." Just leave well enough alone, that's what I thought.

"Well, Ted, I'm still excited about it. I'll be ready. You can count on me. I'm not as good as I used to be, but that's not what's important. What's important is Jack's memory and the pledge." How true.

Dave's reaction was music to my ears. He's still excited! Of the five guys on the team back in 1990, Dave was always in the best shape. Dave had a power ball with incredible spin. His ball would be one board away from the gutter before diving right into the pocket. It was a thing of beauty to see. He did have a knee replaced a year ago, and I was worried he might back out. What a nice surprise. Dave was always our lead off bowler, super consistent, darn near always bowled between 180 and 195.

The only problem with Dave was he was always off talking with someone when it was time for him to bowl. Half the time someone would have to go looking for him. Both teams would be hollering up and down the back area, "hey Dave, you're up." Then, when you did get his attention, he'd saunter back, pick up his ball and wonder what all the fuss was about. Well, he's in on the pledge. That makes three of us. Maybe we'll pull this off after all.

25 years is a long time for a team to wait. There's been a lot of discussion about the last night of bowling and that pledge. Jack made an impressive presentation. He got us all fired up, and he was really good at that. Hope it's all going to be worth it!

More Questions

Matt's the tricky one. He traveled a lot with his job, sometimes overseas for a month at a time. Johnnie always filled in for him. Once in a while, Matt would be called out of town the morning of bowling day, but Johnnie was always ready to fill in. I think Matt agreed to the pledge just to get home that night. Whenever he had a night at home, he was thrilled.

"Hey, Matt, how's it going? What've you been up to?" I dreaded asking Matt that question, so I just stood back.

"Ted, I don't think you really want to know. If you remember, which you probably don't, Amy left me six years ago, and I lost over a $150,000 because of the recession back in 2008." Matt's still Matt.

"Matt, I kind of remember you saying something about that." I never did pay much attention to Matt.

"Yeah, and now I need dentures, my kitchen needs remodeling, the boiler in my house just went out, and now, to top it all off, I've got to use the senior tees when I'm golfing. Everything just seems to be going downhill!" Could Matt be worse than 25 years ago?

"Wow, downhill, huh?" I was never crazy about Matt. Jack liked him, he thought he was smart. I thought he was a jerk, still do. That's about the only thing Jack and I ever disagreed on when it came to the team.

I thought Amy left Matt because he started drinking way too much, and to lose that much cash, well, I can only guess how much he still has left. I think he should have quit golfing six years ago, then again maybe he never should have started. He always was a bellyacher. I think we kept him on the team because we liked it so much when Johnnie subbed for him.

Matt was incredible at keeping score though. He had a way with numbers. In the four years of bowling with him, I never saw a mistake. It can get a little tricky at the end of the last game. He had to add in the handicaps while everyone was standing around waiting to know who won. Being an accountant certainly helped. Matt was thrilled when Corky got those automatic scorekeepers back in 1992.

"Well, Matt, too bad about all the problems. Comes with time, doesn't it? Do you remember the pledge we made with Jack back in 1990 after our last game of the season?" I took a long breath and a deep gulp.

"Sure do, Ted. It was fantastic." Matt could have knocked me over.

I was thrilled when Matt said fantastic, but I had to verify it. "You thought the world of Jack, and for some crazy reason Jack liked you. You seemed to buy into the idea. Do I remember right?" I wondered if I was dreaming.

"You sure do. We were crazy, hey? Jack was acting silly. His thumb was sore as hell. I actually think he may have been a little depressed. He hated that stupid little trophy. I think he wanted to end the season on something that would make us all feel like winners instead of losers." Matt had quite the memory.

"Yeah Matt, that was Jack. He never liked losing. We were a team of winners, that was 'Life according to Jack.'"

"Ted, I still have that dumb little second place black bowling pin. I keep it right on my desk. I think it kept me from ever being a loser again. I think it helped make me the success I am. I'm damn proud of it. What's your take?"

Matt surprised me. I didn't think he was that smart. I suppose he may be successful. Who knows? I just know he lives alone; he drinks way too much, he's a tightwad, has lousy teeth, and always was a crappy golfer. That's what I know about Matt. Jack's friend, not mine.

"Matt, I think you may have nailed it. Jack was our captain, and he carried us so many times. He didn't want us to feel like losers, so he got us all excited about the pledge and none of us could refuse. Now it's time to fulfill the pledge." Now I was getting excited.

The old team's back together, all except Jack. Ready for one more fling! We'll find out if we're still able to work as a team. See if we can make Jack's memory proud.

The Plan

Back in 1990, we were all so young. Anything seemed possible, and Jack could get us fired up about almost anything. We didn't know he was going to die in 2007, at 61 from some health issue.

We thought he'd be around forever. Everyone figured Jack would be the last man standing, and he'd be saluting us.

We all agreed with him that night. We made the pledge together. It made us feel almost invincible, although the drinks didn't hurt either. At his funeral, we all reconfirmed the commitment, just not with the same conviction. Maybe 25 years has taken its toll. Does age sneak up on you overnight and hit you over the head? That's the way it seemed to the team.

You get five guys on the last night of bowling, bowling for first place and drinking together, who knows what might happen. Then you have them lose the match, heck, the whole year, by a lousy 25 pins. Ouch! We needed to feel like winners. Jack knew it. He was our leader. He had to get us all pumped up. So, what did he do?

He came up with this crazy plan. He kept saying, "We're not

going down as losers. We're not going down as losers. We're not going down as losers." He was going to show everybody how good we were, how tough we were, that we weren't losers.

Maybe he was a little tipsy, maybe he did have a few too many. Maybe that metal sliver really did get under his skin. Maybe he was tired of always having to be the hero. That's water over the dam right now. Jack's gone, and now it's up to the four of us. His legacy may be in our hands. It's time for us to put up or shut up. Plain and simple.

I can hear what Jack said to this very day. He stood up there in front of us, all 6-feet, 8-inches of him, and with a grin from ear to ear said, "OK guys, we're not losers! You know what we're going to do to prove it? We're going to sign on to this here '25 Pin Pledge.' We lost by 25 pins, so that's what we'll call it, the '25 Pin Pledge.'"

Then he goes on to explain further.

"Each one of us is going to set aside just $25 a month for 25 years. That's a dollar for each pin, and a year for each pin. I figured it out on this here scratch pad, and that comes to $7,500 each. With five of us, that comes to $37,500."

We were all sitting there thinking, how does this guy's brain work? Who could come up with something like this? What the heck has he been drinking? But at the time, it really sounded kind of neat, and $25 a month wasn't all that much to put aside. Not for a bunch of winners like us.

Then he went on.

"We'll come back here to Corky's on the third Saturday in June of 2015. We'll rent this place for a 25-hour, round the clock bowl-a-thon. We'll donate the money plus any interest to the Children's Hospital, and we really will be winners."

Then he said, "I know it's a long time, but it'll make us feel like champs, and you guys want to feel like champs, right? Remember we're not losers, we're winners, we're champs."

Well none of us could or would argue with him or the plan. It actually sounded inspiring. Jack had a way of doing that. Well, lo and behold, Jack wrote the plan down on the back of our score sheet and had us all sign and date it. No one gave any thought about Corky's being around in 2015, or even if we'd be around, I guess a few drinks can do that.

We thought about starting the bowl-a-thon right after Jack died in 2007. It would have been just 17 years, but 25 seemed important to Jack, so we stuck with the original timeline.

The Big Day

Well, next Saturday is the day. We're all incredibly nervous what with our sore backs, bad knees, and new hips. We stopped bowling as a team the year after Jack died. We just ran out of steam. Maybe that's around the time we all started falling apart. Is it possible the enthusiasm, the excitement, the drive could be generated by one person? If so, it'll be fun to have it all rejuvenated next Saturday, even if it's just for 25 hours!

Jack's old friend Bob, from the Pin Droppers, heard about the plan at Jack's funeral. He mentioned that if we were still up to it when the time came, he and his team would challenge us to a face off. Sort of a 25-hour duel to the finish. He still has three of his teammates around. Turns out Bob and Jack were a whole lot closer than any of us ever knew. I never did see Jack pick Bob up by his ankles, but I'm sure he could have.

Six months ago, Bob suggested both teams start a penny per

pin sponsor drive. That also brought in about $5,000 so far. I also heard, three months ago, that there were 16 teams that wanted to rotate bowling on five-hour shifts. They're also doing the penny per pin sponsor for Jack's memory and Children's Hospital.

Matt figures with what we saved, and the interest it earned, our team should have a little over $75,000 for Children's Hospital. Corky's closed a few years ago, so we rented 16 lanes at a larger bowling house in town. There'll be a lot of hoopla going on for 25 hours, thanks to Jack's memory.

Our sponsor, and substitute bowler Johnnie, had a small bakery back in 1990. Over the years, he expanded into a chain of eight bakeries, and in 2012 a national company bought him out, for a price none of us ever knew. Johnnie and his wife Susan never had any children, and they decided to donate an even $250,000 to Children's Hospital, all in Jack's name.

After Jack's emotional talk back in 1990, Matt, who Jack liked, but I always thought was a jerk, decided to set aside an extra $25 a month. He put it into the stock market, and secretly called it his 'Play money for Jack and the Children's Hospital.' Over the past 25 years, and taking some risky investments, because, as he says, it was 'play money,' it's turned into a little over $75,000. Maybe Matt isn't such a jerk after all.

Jack's youngest sister Claire has a daughter named Heidi that works at a chocolate company as a receptionist. She talked the owner into making a $5,000 contribution to the cause from the company. When he heard about Jack's military service, he personally donated another $20,000 to the Children's Hospital.

It just so happens that Heidi has a new boyfriend who works as a short order cook, at a small-town café about 20 miles from here.

They decided to donate all the proceeds from their Friday night fish-fry to the cause. They figure it should easily come to a little over $2,000.

Jack's older brother Terry knows a fella named Erik who has his own plane. Erik and three of his friends are bringing their planes to the local airfield and giving rides for $25 a person. He also invited a friend named Orville from up north who's bringing his biplane. He'll give rides for $100 a person. They did this a few years ago for a fundraiser, and they raised over $5,000. All this will go to the Children's Hospital, in Jack's name.

Jack was a long-time member of the local VFW Post, and they got all the VFW Posts in our state to join in on the penny-per-pin campaign, plus they'll have six members on site for the 25 hours. They plan on doing some type of raffle during the whole bowl-a-thon. It's anybody's guess as to how much money that may raise.

I guess Jack was really admired! Talk about a true winner.

This whole pledge thing has taken on a magnitude none of us could have ever imagined. It's going to become an annual event. It's going to be called 'Jack's Metal Sliver Bowl-A-Thon.' All the local newspapers and radio stations are promoting it. With Jack's memory, and his choice of Children's Hospital as the cause, the idea has exploded. Matt figures we could easily have over $500,000 to donate to the hospital.

Looking back, who could have ever dreamed that Jack getting a lousy metal sliver in his thumb 25 years ago, could have such a huge impact today?

Maybe our good friend Jack could have.

WHAT IF – Jack's team would have won first place?

Zak's Retirement Dilemma

The Beginning

Shopping at the grocery store and doing laundry used to pop-up on my 'Honey do' list every once in a while, now they're becoming routine. What's up with this retirement thing?

"Zak, when you go to the store later, try to get the smaller lemons, the ones in the stringy bag, they're much juicier. And don't forget to get more of that pink stuff you take for your stomach. I noticed you're running low." I wasn't sure what to say.

"Sure, thing honey, I guess you figure since I retired, I've got nothing else to do but go grocery shopping. Thanks for reminding me about my pink stuff, though." Why is Tanya looking at my pink stuff? Is nothing private after retirement? In the old days I could go a week without using the pink stuff. Now, for some reason, I seem to be taking it more often. I've got to look into that, maybe have our good old family doctor, Doc Johnson, check it out.

"You bet. See you tonight. Don't forget to do the laundry, and this time remember to sort the lights and darks. Love you." I still wasn't sure what to say.

"I'm glad you trust me with the laundry, and by the way, I know how to separate colors, last time was just a fluke. See you later. Have a ball at work and don't get too tired out."

That's what I told Tanya, somewhat tongue in cheek, as she closed the front door and headed off to work. I don't think she heard me. It's probably better that she didn't. She gets a little touchy when I remind her that I'm retired, I think she might be a little jealous. She still has a year and a half to go.

So, there I was, standing at the local Mega Food Store, wondering why the Good Lord put me in this line. I had no idea what was about to happen. How it was going to change the rest of my life. All the new friends I was going to meet, the new experiences I'd have. How was I to know? Maybe that's what's so great about not knowing the future. Trust it to fate.

I had the stringy kind of bag with eight smaller lemons in it, you know, the juicy kind that Tanya wanted. One of those incredibly hard to undo plastic thingamabobs that holds eight small bottles of seltzer water, a plastic container of red grapes, and a bottle of Pepto-Bismol. She said I was running low.

The Bruiser

I was right behind a young fella who was about 6-feet, 6-inches tall, and appeared to be about 260 pounds, which is about 8 inches taller than me and about 60 pounds heavier, but I have about 40 years on him.

In my mind, I nicknamed him 'The Bruiser.'

He was wearing dark blue, very short, cutoff jeans, a white muscle shirt that hardly fit over his biceps, and those shoes with the strap that fits between your first two toes. The sign that reads no shirt, no shoes, no service, forgot to mention socks—oh well. He topped it all off with a blue baseball hat that read, 'Old Guys Rule,' which he had on backwards. Being older, I pay attention to things like that, they kind of bug me. I always wonder, who really are the old guys? But, then again, I am retired.

I had on my loose-fitting gray sweatpants, because my stomach was acting up again. It had been churning ever since that triple cheese and pepperoni pizza the night before. My 4-year-old, worn-out dirty tennis shoes, and a faded grey Iola Old Car Show tee shirt, the one from 2006 with the blue Mustang on the front. I topped it all off with a black baseball hat that I wore correctly, which I got from our oldest granddaughter. It read, 'World's Greatest Grandpa.' I wasn't so sure about that part, but I never questioned her. She's too sweet. I know I didn't look my best, but I was heading to the store with just a quick little list. This was only supposed to be a few minutes in and out. Little did I know.

The Bruiser looked like he could be a linebacker for the Green Bay Packers. He happened to have a shopping cart that was filled up about 4 inches over the top, with things seemingly hanging out over all the sides, and two huge bags of dog food on the bottom rack. We were standing right there in the line that has the big black sign with the big white letters, hanging about 4 feet over our heads, that read, "EXPRESS LANE, APPROX. 15 ITEMS OR LESS." Lucky me. Fun trip.

"Wow, these express lanes sure do make shopping here more convenient. Don't they? I wonder what we did 10 years ago without them, how on earth did we survive?" That's what I said to the petite, barefoot, middle-aged gal with the long flowing black hair, in the tight, bright yellow spandex outfit. She was standing in the aisle right next to me. She was holding a watermelon and a bottle of vodka. I let my mind wander.

"Sure do, I suppose." That was her entire response. I think she was frowning at me, but I didn't want to gawk. My mind continued to wander.

I had said it in a rather quiet, but disgusted voice. I must have been a little too quiet, because the Bruiser never flinched. I guess maybe I was lucky, but my stomach was starting to churn, again. After that, I kept quiet. I just stood there smiling. The lady in yellow never really did pay any attention to me, I think she was too enamored with the Bruiser. In a way I didn't blame her, I kind of was also. He was a sight to behold.

The Flirt

The Bruiser finally got his cart up next to the conveyor belt. Then this incredibly beautiful, young woman who was working the checkout machine said, in a rather provocative voice, "Hi there, honey. Were you able to find everything you needed, or is there anything else you'd like?"

The Bruiser seemed to blush and somewhat squirm. He appeared to be uncomfortable. I was amazed. He looked back at me with a puzzled look on his face, smiled at her and said, "No thanks, I found everything my wonderful wife had on the list. I even added the two boxes of cereal that our daughters were talking about yesterday morning at breakfast."

I was impressed with his response. He was a family man, and he let her know. My stomach quieted down somewhat, but I did wonder what was going through his mind. Does this happen to him often? What are his wife and kids like? Where does he come from? I shop here fairly often, and I've never seen him before. There's always something new to think about, to create more stress and tension. Like that's what I needed right then.

They chit-chatted for what seemed like an eternity, although it was more like a minute or two. I stood there looking at that little pink bottle, thinking to myself, "Now I know why someone invented this stuff." I guess I'm not the only one who lives with stress and tension.

The Bruiser started unloading his cart, when about six cans of what looked like dog food fell out and rolled under his cart. The beautiful young check out gal and the lady in the yellow spandex outfit just about got whiplash watching as the Bruiser started crawling around trying to catch the runaway cans of dog food. It was a sight to behold. I don't remember who I was watching more, the guy with the short shorts, or the two-gals gawking. The episode completely took my mind off of where I was, the Mega Food Store, the express lane, and my stomach. I believe I relaxed for the moment.

I started counting what I had: a sack of eight lemons, eight small bottles of seltzer water, a plastic container of grapes, and that bottle of Pepto-Bismol, you know, just in case. I had over 15 items. Should I quietly move to another lane, should I put back the red grapes? Heck no, I was going to stand my ground. I wanted to hear that provocative voice from that beautiful young checkout gal.

The lemons I had were for our daily glass of lemon water. It's fantastic at cleaning out our digestive system, at least according to our youngest daughter. The seltzer water goes with the brandy I drink the night before. That doesn't help my situation, but then I have a good reason to clean out my system, at least that's what I figure. I'm not sure what the red grapes are for. Maybe they help Tanya feel better about drinking red wine.

The pink stuff is for my stomach. I taught English at the local high school for almost 30 years. I loved it most of the time, and I only had a handful of kids that were difficult. One kid named Frank said he was going to kill me. He flunked English and I wouldn't let him get his diploma until, with the help of a tutor, he passed the exam during summer school. That was 20 years ago. I never had an issue with my stomach until that day.

"You know Zak, you might have an ulcer, or it could be stress, or something else. Whatever it is, it's something we've got to deal with. For now, take one of these pills twice a day and we'll check it in one month." That's what Doc Johnson told me a week ago.

I didn't like the 'or something else.' My mind went to all kinds of other problems.

I just think it's that I miss the routine of teaching, the activity, the comradery. Seeing the excitement on the kids' faces when they aced an English test was always a thrill. Well, maybe not Frank. He was a tough one, he never aced one of my tests. After 30 years of doing the same thing you get familiar with it, it becomes comfortable. All I know is I miss it. Now I'm waiting in the Express Line at the Mega Food Store and doing laundry—go figure.

The Bruiser was about halfway through his cart when I started thinking about how Mom used to send me down to the corner grocery store to get lemons, so she could make lemon meringue pies. Boy, did I love those pies.

Memories

60 years later, and I can still hear my Mom asking, "Zak, honey, where are the lemons?"

"Huh? What lemons?" I guess I was always a little off kilter.

"The lemons I sent you to the store for. They were at the top of the list I gave you." I was impressed that I didn't lose the list, and now mom's hollering at me. What gives?

"Oh, cremini, I ran into Little Gary and he told me about a water balloon fight in Fat Johnnies backyard in 15 minutes. I totally forgot the lemons. Sorry."

"Well then, you'd better get down to the store and get back with those lemons in 10 minutes. Honestly, you're the most forgetful person I know, except maybe your father."

I was pretty absentminded, even as a kid, and that kind of conversation with my mom happened more than I liked to remember. I ran to the store down on the corner, all the while thinking about the water balloon fight, and then I ran into Mr. Meyer. "Zachariah, how nice to see you back so soon. You look like you were running. What's going on? Are you in a rush?"

"I'm in a really big hurry Mr. Meyer. I need four lemons, the nice juicy kind. Mom's making a lemon pie for desert tonight, and I kinda, well sorta forgot, well anyway I'm in a really big hurry, Mr. Meyer." Sometimes Mr. Meyer could talk for hours, at least that's the way it always seemed to me.

"Ok, Zachariah. I'll get them for you. Now don't you forget, you have to be here at four o'clock sharp to carry all those soda pop bottles down to the basement. Remember, you have a job here. Right?" Good old Mr. Meyer. He gave me my first job. I carried soda bottles down the steps, and into the basement storage area. He paid me with candy bars. What a memorable first job.

"Yes, yes, yes, Mr. Meyer, I won't forget. Not about my new job, no way, I'll be here right at four. I'm not that forgetful." I probably was.

Back then, I actually thought the only thing lemons were good for was making lemon meringue pies. I always figured lemonade was for girls and sissies, but I was only 10.

The grocery store was across the street and down on the corner of Fifth and Main Street. It was owned by Frank and Margaret Meyer. They owned the store for over 25 years, and they knew everybody in the neighborhood. They had to close after the huge chain store came into town, up on the north side. They never had any kids, so they always enjoyed all of us kids, even Evil Emil.

Back in Line

While the Bruiser's cart was slooooowly being emptied, I started reminiscing about the old Eighth Street gang from 60 years ago. There was Little Gary, Fat Johnnie, Smooth Larry, Fast Gene, Cutie Pie Matt, Evil Emil, and some other guys I can't even remember. We ranged from 9 years old up to 12 years old—some old guys, and some great memories. Great time to grow up, even with Evil Emil.

I remembered the baseball games in the alley, kick the can, tag, bike races, and wrestling matches, which Evil Emil always won. I was the victim of that ordeal way more than once. I don't think anybody ever got the better of Evil Emil. I do remember one time, though. It was when Fast Gene told Evil Emil, "Hey Evil Emil, you can't catch me, you're too fat, you're fatter than Fat Johnnie." Wow was that a mistake.

"I'm gonna catch you, and when I do, I'm gonna pound you into a peanut shell. Your sister can't help you this time, not like last time, you'd better look out. I'm gonna smack you a good one."

Well Evil Emil caught Fast Gene, we all knew he would, and the rest is what 'Local Legends' are made of. Emil had Gene in a headlock and was rubbing the heck out of Gene's head, he may have even pulled out some hair, we never did know for sure. Gene started crying and screaming. Lo and behold, Gene's sister came out of the next-door backyard. She was 15 and extra-large, to say the least. Well she took into Evil Emil with both hands swinging. Emil had blood coming out of his mouth, nose, and one ear. He let go of Gene, started cussing, and took off down the alley like a bullet.

Gene's sister Sally became the hero for all of us. We all thought she was who they made the cartoon Wonder Woman about. Gene recovered fine; all his bleeding stopped by that night. Emil lost his nickname 'Evil' and we didn't see him for three weeks. After that he was just one of the guys. It was kind of nice, not being afraid of Emil anymore.

I have fond memories of those old days, the guys, Mom's lemon meringue pies, the corner grocery stores. They had absolutely everything you could want. If they were out of something, the next one over would have it. If you wanted Cheerios, they had them. If you wanted Triscuits, they had them; toothpaste, they had it; toilet paper, they had it. Mr. Meyer was the best of them at keeping his shelves fully stocked.

While I was standing in line behind the Bruiser, I started thinking how in these Mega Food Stores, if you want Cheerios, they have 15 different kinds. Triscuits, there are 20 different varieties; toothpaste, each manufacturer makes 10 different styles; toilet paper—don't even get me started. They could fit Mr. Meyer's entire store into the produce section of this Mega Food Store. 60 years ago, we didn't need all the different selections. Maybe life was easier back then. I never had any stomach issues those days, but I was just 10. I guess now I'm supposed to be older and wiser.

Check Out
The Bruiser had a few items left, and I was beginning to get back to reality when some kid behind me said, in a rather loud

obnoxious voice, "Hey, Dude, when life gives you lemons, make lemonade." That did it. I thought, 'Lemonade is for girls, I'm no girl and I'm certainly not a sissy.' I was getting ready to grab that little pink bottle, and open it and have a swig, when I heard the computer cash register spitting out the receipt.

The Bruiser's bill was $238.79, then he pulled out a disorganized wad of coupons. The beautiful young check out gal, sorted carefully and slowly through them all and got it down to $194.32. The Bruiser was all smiles, thanked her and headed out the door. I got through the checkout line with no problem. I took my meager belongings and headed out to my car. I happened to walk by the Bruiser while he was loading all those funny little plastic bags into his neat little Volvo station wagon.

His wagon had those bumper stickers on it with sayings like "Go Green – Save the Planet," "Recycle – for the Planet's Safety," and one of those cute little "Coexist" stickers with the funny letters. That's always been my favorite, just ahead of "I Like Ike." I stopped, looked over at him, and said in a rather disgusted voice, "Have a great day fella, hope you weren't in any hurry." The Bruiser looked up from loading his bags of groceries, smiled and said, "Thanks friend, you too!"

Looking back, if I would have had a crystal ball earlier in the day, I never would have been in the express lane. I would have gone into another line and never met the Bruiser. The memories I never would have thought about. And now, I may have a new friend.

WHAT IF – Zak wouldn't have stayed in the EXPRESS LANE ?

Zak's English Lesson

The Father & Son

"Hey, dude, when life gives you lemons, make lemonade."

That's what the kid in the back of the Express Lane at the Mega Food Store said that life changing morning. Geeze, that really got under my skin. I waited a few seconds before I turned around to see who the wise guy was. I wasn't in the best of humor right then; the Bruiser and the beautiful young check out gal had just about popped my cork. My mind was someplace else. My stomach had been churning because of that triple cheese and pepperoni pizza the night before. I wasn't sure if I should take the pink stuff or find some brandy. I was kind of fried.

Happy shopping.

Holy Cow, it was Jimmy, Frank's kid. Frank, the kid I almost flunked in English class 20 years ago. Good grief! Why him? Then the kid goes and smiles at me, with that kind of smirky smile you'd like to put a sock in. He knew exactly who I was. I wondered what he was thinking about, what made him say that. He couldn't have any idea what I think about lemonade. Did he think I was a sissy? Did his dad, Frank, tell him something? Did they know I had a weakness, that I was vulnerable?

When he said that, I was stuck in the express lane. I was right behind the Bruiser and his now, half-empty grocery cart. A young girl with a package of Twinkies was right behind me. She was working away on her cell phone, totally oblivious to anything going on around her. And Jimmy was right behind her. The lady in the bright yellow spandex outfit was just checking out next to us. Happy, happy shopping.

I had both Jimmy and his dad Frank in my English class. Jimmy graduated last year, and Frank, with a lot of help from me and a tutor, graduated 20 years ago. Someone once said, "An acorn doesn't fall far from the tree." In my mind, truer words were never spoken. This must have been a family of acorns, and I wondered how many generations it may have covered. The only redeeming thing was that Jimmy was a tad, but just a tad, smarter than his dad. Jimmy did it all on his own. Thank goodness!

His dad Frank was my nemesis. Jimmy was his protégé. Imagine that. Frank really wasn't such a bad kid, even though he did threaten to kill me. He just hated English class. He hated that it was the last class of the day, and he hated that he had a front row seat. He also hated that his good buddies were all in the back of the classroom. And so, it went without saying—he hated me. He's the kid that started calling me Mr. Z.

In 20 years, I'll never forget the look on his face when he walked into my classroom that first day and saw the seating assignment.

"Mr. Z, I can't sit up here. Don't you know I'm claustrophobic? It runs in my family. Didn't anyone in the front office ever tell you?" I was stunned.

"Frank, no the front office never said anything about you being claustrophobic. Anyway, it would be worse in the back of the room." One of Franks good buddies cheered when I said that.

Then I heard, "Mr. Z, another thing, about my hearing. When

you write on the blackboard it makes my brain go bananas. That sound goes through me like lightning."

"Frank, you're just going to have to live with it for now. I gave out the seating assignments according to everyone's last names, and this is where you came out. You'll be fine up here." I wasn't about to give in to some kid.

Then he says, "No way, I'll never make it up here for the whole year. I just know I won't."

"Frank, tell you what, as soon as you get a B plus on one of my exams, I'll move you to a middle row. But for now, just try to concentrate." I told him that with a bit of a smile on my face. You could say it was the beginning of an incredibly fascinating relationship.

The only time he looked meaner was when I wouldn't let him graduate and get his diploma. After some very intense conversations with him, his father Wilfred, and our school principal, I caved in. He was allowed to put on his cap and gown and walk across the stage with the rest of his classmates, however he did receive a blank diploma. He wasn't thrilled with that, but it was a compromise.

"Frank, you've been coming to my class for a whole semester. The best grade you ever got was a D minus, and you did that just one time. I've warned you for three weeks this was going to happen." Why is it that some guys just never believe?

"Well Mr. Z, you know I'm not the sharpest knife in the drawer. What the hell did you want me to do, cheat? I may be stupid, but I don't cheat." I gave him credit for being honest.

"Frank, I've never called you stupid, I may have wondered about your grasp of the English language sometimes, but I've never called you stupid. For some crazy reason, you just thought everybody graduates. You didn't seem to realize you have to work at it." I tried pushing the work ethic because I knew how well he did in all of his shop classes. He was the best in his wood shop class, straight A's.

"Mr. Z, if you would have put me in the back of the room, with my buddies, I know I could have passed English class." I thought: yeah, but what about your buddies?

"Frank, you need to get a diploma in order to get a decent, good paying, job. You're not going to have your buddies around all the time to help you out. You need to do it on your own." I think Frank was sweating.

"Yeah, but, if you don't pass me, I don't know what I'll do. Either I'm going to kill you, or my dad will. One of us will run you down if we have to. I'm totally freaked out. What can I do?"

I tried to calm him down, "Frank, I'll tell you what I can do. I'll let you wear your graduation cap and gown and walk across the stage with all your classmates. You can smile and laugh with them and be the goof-off you always like to be."

"Good, my buddies will like that. It might be fun." Now he was smiling.

"OK Frank, but after graduation your family has to hire a tutor and you have to get at least a D on the same final exam you just had." That was my ultimatum.

"I can do that, no problem." He was full of unwarranted confidence.

"You'll have one month after graduation. You do that, and you can have your real diploma."

Boy, Frank was ticked. I heard his buddies really needled him about it. His one buddy Joey even offered to be his tutor. Joey passed with a C minus—great tutor he would have been. I never told anybody anything, I just waited to see what would happen next.

His dad, Wilfred, must have called me a dozen times. It got so bad I was always hesitant to answer the phone after seven at night. Wilfred was downright hostile. I've dealt with disappointed parents before, but this was a whole new experience. I'm not sure most of his words were even in the English language. That's when I bought my first bottle of the pink stuff. Right after Wilfred's first call.

Frank's Grandma hired a tutor. She was the saint in the family. She came to me one day and asked about Joey being his tutor. I guess she never met Joey. She and I agreed Joey was out, so she settled on the young man who was my teacher's aide. Frank studied his butt off according to my aide, and he never cheated. He wound up getting a C minus. I completely expected at least a straight C, since it was the exact same test as a month before, but I was just the teacher. My aide was disappointed, and he wanted Frank to try again, but I reminded him about Frank's dad, Wilfred. Enough said.

Time for Some Fun

After getting home from the store and thinking about Jimmy and his Dad Frank, and his Granddad Wilfred, I needed some relaxation. I needed to take my mind off the fiasco that went on back then. After putting my stuff away, I started thinking about *When Life gives you Lemons, make Lemonade*. Curious how the mind works. Tanya and I have been making lemon water for years. Without sugar, it isn't lemonade. Jimmy left out the word sugar, but that's Jimmy, Frank's kid.

Then I got to thinking about all those old sayings that sound so neat. Do they really mean anything? Did they ever make any sense?

Since I'd just been at the Mega Food Store, the first thing that came to my mind was *Getting a Bakers Dozen*. I wondered what that was all about. I've bought a lot of rolls, doughnuts, and muffins, but I was never offered 13 of anything. How come?

I decided to look it up. Turns out the idea goes back to the 12th and 13th centuries, when bread was sold more by weight than by items. Bakers added an extra loaf of bread, so they wouldn't be fined or even flogged for selling bread that was underweight.

Thinking about bread, the next thing I wondered about was *buttering someone up*. What was that all about? Turns out it was an ancient Indian custom to throw balls that were similar to butter, and had a great taste, at the statues of gods in order to seek their favor. I wondered if that would work with Tanya.

Being in the bakery frame of mind, I wondered about *eating humble pie*. Well, that refers to eating the entrails of deer which were baked into a pie and served to the servants of the household. Now I wondered—why were they so mistreated while some in the household were *born with a silver spoon in their mouth*? That was a reference to grandparents gifting silver spoons to their grandchildren when they were christened.

Thinking about grandparents, I stumbled on the phrase *dirt poor*. Turns out my great-grandparents must have fit that description. It referred to those who could only afford to have dirt floors in their cottages. The wealthier folks had wood floors. I wondered about dirt floors and what happens when it rains and gets all sloppy and muddy. Did it ever *rain cats and dogs*?

My favorite explanation for this is that back when most homes had thatched roofs, which was thick straw piled high, the best place for smaller street animals, like cats and dogs to go to keep warm, was up on those roofs. When it rained quite hard, the roofs would get very slippery, and sometimes the animals would slip off the roofs, and it would literally be raining cats and dogs. Go figure.

Now, Tanya was starting to wonder about me.

She started to wonder if I *got out of the wrong side of the bed* this morning. She started giving me *the cold shoulder*, and was almost wishing I'd *kick the bucket*. I asked Tanya if *the cat got her tongue* because I *caught her red handed*, staring at me. I was *pleased as punch*.

By this time, I figured I'd *rubbed her the wrong way* long enough. I knew I was *flying by the seat of my pants*, so I'd better get back *on the straight and narrow* before I had to *eat crow*. Well, by now, Tanya knew I had *bitten off more than I could chew*, and that I was *barking up the wrong tree*. Tanya really didn't want to go *cold turkey* on me because she knew I was just *pulling her leg*.

Suddenly the doorbell rang, and we were both *saved by the bell*. We both had an incredibly good laugh before I went to answer the door. We decided we were both *coexisting* quite nicely. It was a great afternoon, what could possibly go wrong?

Guess

Much to my surprise, it was Frank and Jimmy at the door.

"Tanya, would you please get me my bottle of that pink stuff? It's in the bathroom medicine cabinet. I think I just bought a new bottle." My mind was racing.

"What's the deal? We were having such a good time laughing and kidding around. Did you get a stomach cramp or something?" Tanya sounded confused.

"I think maybe it's something! Just bring the pink stuff, please." I said that with a rather sober tone.

"Hello, Frank and Jimmy, what can I do for you?" I was cautious to say the least.

Jimmy said, "Mr. Z, I, ah, I, think ah, I'm not, ah. Oh heck."

"Jimmy, what's up?" I didn't want to stare.

"Mr. Z, I'd like to, ah, I mean, I should. Mr. Z, maybe if, ah." He was stuttering.

"Jimmy, what the heck is going on?" Now I was staring, he had my complete attention.

"I really am ah, the lemons and water, I really, ah. At the store this morning, I, ah maybe. Oh, dang it."

"Jimmy, you're not making much sense. I'm having a hard time understanding what you're trying to tell me. Can I do something for you?" I was starting to get a little concerned, and my gut was getting warm.

Jimmy looked like he had been sweating. He had changed his clothes since I saw him in the Mega Food Store this morning. He got out of his sweats and into a nice-looking outfit. He looked better than I've seen him look in three or four months. He was holding something strange in his right hand. I told Tanya she'd better wait in the kitchen.

Then, out of nowhere, Jimmy stopped talking and started crying. I had no idea what was going on. I was speechless. I asked again if there was anything I could do, and Jimmy calmed down somewhat. I heard the word sorry, but I couldn't understand anything else he said. I knew he passed English. I knew he could talk. After all, he got a C minus. I was stunned!

Then Frank gave Jimmy a little shove and said, "Tell him what I told you. This has been going on way too long, now tell him. Speak up! Don't be a wienie."

Jimmy spoke up, "Mr. Z, I'm sorry for being such a wise guy at the store this morning. I didn't mean to upset you. I was just trying to be funny. I thought maybe you'd get a kick out of it. I'm sorry."

Good grief. Is this Jimmy? I was blown away, still speechless. Then Frank chimed in.

"Zak, Jimmy came home this morning and told me about what he said to you at the store. He said you looked upset with him. He said he thought it was funny, but you looked mad. I think maybe it's time we straighten out this mess. 20 years is a long time, and I think it's mainly my fault."

My mind was slowly beginning to function. Frank and Jimmy are standing in front of me, looking like two little kids who were just sent into a time-out. Sorry and guilty, both at the same time. I needed to wake up. I'm not sure if I was scared, nervous, or just plain dumbfounded.

"Well, Frank, it has been a long time. I know you've become very successful and have the best woodworking shop in town. I've followed your career ever since you graduated. I even sat in the back of church at your wedding, I'm quite pleased with your progress. I'm actually quite proud of you and your family. What's up?"

The three of us had a nice, long conversation. Frank admitted neither he nor his father, Wilfred, ever intended to do me any harm. I was pretty sure, or somewhat sure, I always knew that. He explained that when his cousin almost ran me over when I was on my bike 18 years ago it was a total accident. It was kind of my fault. I had a dark outfit on, and it was getting pretty dark outside. I should have had reflectors or a light on, at least that's what his cousin thought. Not too bright on my part.

He said how when his dad, Wilfred, took off my driver's side front car door 16 years ago, it was because I really wasn't looking before I opened it. I admitted that really was my fault, but I really was concerned that day. I remember to this day the excited look on Wilfred's face. He was almost smiling. At least that's the way I saw it. Frank admitted he was completely at fault for not passing English in his senior year. He actually thanked me for the second chance. He said my teacher's aide was fantastic, and he never could have done it without his help.

Jimmy opened up. "Mr. Z, I always thought you were the fairest teacher I had in senior year. You knew I wasn't any good at English, but you did the best you could with me. I never really believed my dad when he said you had a mean streak. I figured you were just concerned about your students."

Then he handed me the thing he had in his right hand. It was an 8-inch tall cross that he made in his dad's woodshop. It was gorgeous, and it looked exactly like an old wooden cross would look. It even had little holes where the nails would have been. On the back he had inscribed, "Mr. Z, thanks for your help."

"Well, Frank and Jimmy, you've left me kind of speechless. For an English teacher that's rather hard to do. I appreciate the both of you coming over here to try and straighten this whole thing out. It's very gratifying."

"Well, Zak. I thought it was time." Coming from Frank, that kind of blew my mind.

"It has been a long time, Frank. I probably should have moved you to the middle of the room, or laid down the law after the first week, but I just let it drag on too long. Sorry."

Just then, Tanya came in from the kitchen and, of all things, she offered us some lemonade! She swore she had no idea what we were talking about. The three of us just smiled at her. The, "yeah sure you didn't," kind of smile.

It probably never really started, but now it's all over. Three guys and Wilfred's spirit, (Wilfred passed away two years ago—I went to his funeral, just to be sure), are now coexisting very nicely. That's a nice word. Maybe we need more of it in the world today. At least that's what I thought anyway.

All this because of standing in the wrong line at the right time, or then again, maybe the right line at the wrong time. Now I have three new friends, The Bruiser, Frank, and Jimmy. My list keeps growing.

It's a great life after all!

WHAT IF – Jimmy would have gone into a different line?

Zak Coexisting in New York

What?

"Zak, I have to get over to the care center right away. Kathy had her baby last night, and they need someone to fill in for her. You're on your own for lunch today. I should be home around six, I'll do supper after I get home. Love you!"

That's what I heard while I was in the middle of shaving this morning. I cut my lower lip, right in the area that never wants to stop bleeding. Dang it. Why didn't Tanya come into the room and explain what was going on? Why did she just holler down the hallway? I never was any good at last minute changes. You never know what's going to happen. Sometimes it really upsets my stomach, must be the nerves, I hope. If I knew ahead of time, maybe I'd be OK, but…oh well!

Finally, I had a great night's sleep. I never thought about Frank, Jimmy, Wilfred's spirit, or English classes, not once, not all night. A huge storm came through here last night. There were hundreds of lightning bolts with all the accompanying thunder, at least that's what Tanya said. I slept right through the whole ordeal. She was a little ticked that I never woke up, she said I missed all the fun and excitement. I don't think so. I've seen storms before, and I had enough fun and excitement yesterday to last quite a while. Right now, I feel great.

The front passed, the storm's over, and the sun's shining. As someone once said, "It's a beautiful day in the neighborhood." No doubt about it. There must have been at least an inch and a half of rain last night. Now the ground is drenched, the trees are dripping, and the birds are singing.

It's going to be a great day. I hope.

The Tricky Mind

"Tanya, where's the milk? I can't find it in the fridge. I didn't even get a kiss or a chance to say goodbye this morning. I cut my dang lip shaving and got blood all over the sink, and all I heard was you mumbling something down the hall. Why did you say you were leaving?" I probably shouldn't have sounded so absentminded.

"Zak, Dear! I told you Kathy had her baby. You called me at work just to ask about milk? You've got to be kidding me. You must have been half asleep when I left." Tanya sounded upset, I wondered why.

"I wasn't asleep, I was shaving! Now what about the milk?" I could get upset also.

"Don't you remember? I told you yesterday, we're out of milk. You'll have to get some at the store. Before you go, check and see what else we might need, there's also a list on the fridge. I'm glad you need me, but try to make it on your own today, and stop being so forgetful. Love you."

I shot back, "Tanya, wait a minute, what do you mean forgetful? You think my memory's going? You're the nurse, what do you think?" I was getting kind of concerned. Dealing with my stomach was one thing, but now she has me worried about my memory. Maybe I shouldn't have retired.

"Zak, have you ever heard about senior moments? Don't worry, and I'll see you around six. I've got some real issues to deal with over here. I've got to go. Love you." Then she hung up on me.

Mr. Forgetful

I just got back from the Mega Food Store, what a great morning for a walk. I got my Cheerios. I get them because of what Grandma told me 60 years ago, "Eat your Cheerios because they're good for your heart." Then my Grandpa would always say "Zak, always remember that whatever Grandma says is God's honest truth." How could I not believe them? They truly were the greatest.

I did, however, switch to Honey Nut Cheerios about 20 years ago. I'm sure Grandma wouldn't have minded; she probably would have done the same thing. Grandma's the person who got me interested in the English language. She talked me into becoming a teacher, she wanted me to follow in her footsteps. Grandma had great taste, at least that's what Grandpa always said.

I also picked up some blueberries, some bananas, and on a whim, I decided to get one of my old favorites, Frosted Flakes. The kind Tony the Tiger loved. They're GR-R-REAT! I spent at least three minutes looking for the old-fashioned kind, the original ones. There were four shelves at least ten feet long full of frosted flakes, all with different brands and flavors. Mine were right next to the garlic flavored frosted flakes. Must be a health thing, I'll have to ask our daughter.

I started putting everything away and was about to have a bowl of the Frosted Flakes, when I discovered that I forgot the milk. How could I forget the milk? That's the main thing that I went for. Why didn't I make a shopping list? What's wrong with me? Hopefully it's that senior moment thing, I sure hope Tanya's right.

I figured I may as well go back to the store, only this time I'll write MILK on a slip of paper and stick it in my wallet and paper clip it to my money. No forgetting it again. It was too nice of a day to waste inside, and much too wet outside to do yard work, so it was a great day for a walk.

Down through the brand-new condo complex, past their Olympic size pool and club house. Then through a corner of the best park in the county, and alongside a meandering creek running the entire length of the 18th fairway. Up through the church cemetery past all the old tombstones from the mid 1800s. Finally, across the street and through the bank's driveway, right into the Mega Food Store's huge parking lot. 20 minutes tops, unless I see some white tail deer in the county park, then it's time to take pictures.

Once inside the Mega Food Store it's another long walk back to the milk section. When I was a 10-year old kid, I crossed the street, walked four houses down to the corner grocery store and bought milk. Now that I'm retired, I walk three-quarters of a mile to get milk. What's up with all that?

I got into the store, got my milk, and found that same beautiful young gal that checked out the Bruiser. She was working that express lane again.

"So, how do you like working here? I imagine it can get a little hectic sometimes. You know, people coming through your EXPRESS LANE, APPROX. 15 ITEMS OR LESS, with way too many items. Must make it tough occasionally." That's what I asked her, anxiously awaiting her reply.

"Huh? What do you mean?" It looked as if her eyes were closed.

"See that sign hanging right above my head?" I pointed straight up.

"Oh, that old thing. I never pay any attention to that. I don't have time to count what people have. That's not my job. I do like working here though, I meet some really neat guys, usually." I wasn't sure if that was a dig on me or not, so I just smiled.

The Meeting

As I left the store with my half gallon of almond milk, I walked right past, well, almost right past, the Bruiser. The fella that was in front of me in the express lane a month ago. He had that shopping cart filled up over the brim and two huge bags of dog food. I thought about accidently pushing a shopping cart into his cute little Volvo station wagon, but he is about 8 inches taller than me and about 60 pounds heavier. As someone else once said, "Discretion is the better part of valor."

The Bruiser was loading more of those silly plastic bags filled with stuff into his cute little station wagon, the one with the "Coexist" bumper sticker on the back. I was going to just pass by him, but then I thought, heck no, I'm going to confront him. I'm going to find out who he is, and where he's from.

"Hey, fella. Nice wagon. I really like that neat little "Coexist" bumper sticker on the back. You kind of follow that philosophy when you're shopping? Did you put it on there, or was it on there when you bought that cute little wagon? I also like your bumper sticker about saving the planet by using more paper bags. Sounds like a good idea to me. What do you think?"

I thought those two little digs might have been a little too much. I figured I was in the middle of the huge Mega Food Store parking lot, what could he do to me out here? He doesn't know where I live, I'm safe.

"Hey, friend. I remember you from a month ago. You're the poor dude that had to stand behind me when I was in the wrong line." He straightened up and I remembered the 8-inch difference in height.

"Yep, that was me alright." I sort of gulped.

"I never did notice that sign till the next time I was in the store. I really am sorry. I know it took a long time for me to get through that line, but if you remember, the check-out gal didn't help. She had me kind of bedazzled."

Bedazzled, I hadn't heard that word in ages, I was puzzled.

"Well, she sure was something else. I thought she was kind of cute myself. How about you?" I figured it was time to push him a little.

"I thought she was cute but a little too pushy. Hey, I'd like to treat you to a cup of coffee, but right now I'm running late. I've got to get all this stuff over to the food pantry. Sorry! Maybe next time?" He said that while he was putting the last pink plastic bag into his Volvo.

He took me off guard, I wasn't sure if he was talking about THE food pantry or HIS food pantry. He was hard to read! I decided to go out on a limb and pursue the idea. I had more time than money right then.

"Yeah, sounds like a plan. Maybe next time. I shop here a lot; and my wife always has a list for me. I seem to get here fairly often; I'm usually forgetting something or another. Next time I see you, I'll remind you." I really didn't plan on reminding him, and I thought I may never see him again. Actually, I hoped I would never see him again.

Then his phone started ringing. He answered it and said, "No kidding. I thought you had to have all this stuff by noon, and now you don't need it till three. OK, fine by me. You're the boss." He looked at me, and said his plans had changed, and how would I like to get a cup of coffee. On him. The Mega Food store has a neat coffee bar inside with loads of choices. How could I refuse?

"Sure, my milk's good for a while. How about all your stuff in those neat little pink plastic bags? You know, all the stuff for the pantry." I said that with one of those questioning looks on my face, you know, where you scrunch up your eyebrows.

"It's all nonperishable. You know how the food pantry works. Right? They won't take anything that can spoil, and this is all good." That answered my question about the food pantry or his pantry.

We visited for about a half hour. Turns out he is married, hence the shopping list from his wife last month. That's why he made such a big point that day to the beautiful young gal in the checkout lane. He mentioned his list from his wife, and that he has two daughters.

He introduced himself as Max, which was my Grandfather's name. Grandpa passed away almost 40 years ago. Tanya and I still visit the family gravesites a couple times a year to place flowers. Makes me feel good. It helps keep my stomach calm, and Tanya likes to dig in the dirt.

Coexisting

"Well Max, my name is Zak. So, about that "Coexist" bumper sticker, did you put it on or was it there when you bought the car?" I was getting kind of nosey, I wanted to keep pushing.

His eyes lit up, "heck yes, I put it on. My wife bought the car new just three years ago. I love that bumper sticker. I bought a dozen of them when I was going to college in New York City. I put them on all the cars we own. I like the idea of coexisting. Neat, huh? What do you think?"

"Well Max, I like the idea of coexisting a whole lot. As a matter of fact, I just had an incredible coexisting experience with two former students. It's way more than you want to hear about, but it really was nice. Gives you faith in humanity, if you know what I mean." I was guessing he knew.

"I sure do. Working with humanity is somewhat my gig." He had me confused. I wanted to dislike him. I thought he'd been rude a month ago, but he did mention his wife and daughters to the check-out gal. That was rather decent. I thought he was way too large for that silly little Volvo. I thought his muscle shirt, cut-off jeans, and that stupid hat that said, 'Old Guys Rule,' were all dumb. I thought none of his colors matched, and his shoes were crazy, if you even call them shoes. He called me 'friend' that day, and I thought, who the heck does he think he is?

"So, your name is Max. Interesting, that was my grandfather's name. He was a great guy. He was a deputy sheriff up north back in the early 1900s."

"Wow, that had to be an interesting job. I bet he ran into some moonshiners up there. What about your Grandma?" I thought nice question, shows concern.

"Well, Grandpa and Grandma also had a huge farm with 93 milking cows and every kind of crop you could think of. They ran it until Gramps was 84. Great man, salt of the earth kind of guy. He was a fantastic role model for me. What about yourself?" Another little push.

"Well Zak, your Grandpa sounds like a tough act to follow. Don't think I'm capable. I wouldn't even try." Max was sitting on the edge of his stool, like my Grandfather used to do. It made me think of Gramps with a smile. I wasn't sure if this was some kind of con game Max was playing, or if he was for real. Now, I even wondered if he was married with two daughters. He was beginning to sound a little too slick for me.

"So, tell me more about yourself and your family. You said you have two girls at home?" I had to push and push some more.

He came right back, "yes, I have a wife, a five-year-old daughter named Joy, and a three-year-old daughter named Valerie. Here's a picture of them."

"Lovely girls. What about your wife, what does she do?" She was much prettier than the check-out gal.

"Her name is Shirley. She's what's called a stay at home mom, and she loves it. She does sell a little Mary Kay product on the side, but there's no pink Cadillac yet." His eyes lit up again and his smile went from ear to ear.

"Nice Max. What about yourself?" I kept pushing.

He kept coming right back with the correct answers "Me? Oh, I'm a teacher up at the high school on the north side of town. I've been there three years."

"Nice. What do you teach?" I felt like I was pulling teeth.

"Oh, I teach social studies. I'm also the assistant football coach. I was hired with the unwritten stipulation that when the head coach retires in three years, I'd be first in line for that position."

I thought that was interesting. I was getting somewhat comfortable with Max, so I said, "I think Volvo's really are neat little cars and, being my age, I really have a fondness for station wagons. We always had one when we had our kids, but you're a bit large for that. Don't you think?"

Max chuckled. He said it really is a tight fit for him, but he's the only one who will drive it fast enough to keep the engine cleaned out. Shirley just drives it around town when she goes out with

Mary Kay products. Max likes to open it up out on the highway. He says he likes to get it up to 70 for half an hour or so.

"You said you went to college in New York. Tell me more about that. Tanya and I lived in Manhattan for a year, a few years ago." I was feeling comfortable with Max, I decided I could share that with him.

"Zak, you're kidding. What in the world made you and Tanya move there, and why in the world did you come back here?" He stood up and moved his baseball cap around the right way, I was impressed.

"Well, Max, we really enjoyed the city, but you obviously know how expensive it can get." I left it at that and asked about that "Co-exist" sticker one more time.

"Zak, I think New York City is the perfect example of coexisting. In the five years I went to school there, all I ever saw was coexisting. Everybody was too busy with their own life to bother anybody else."

"Max, I couldn't agree more."

I was beginning to like this guy; the slickness was going away. By now, I believed Max never did see that high hanging sign. He apologized, and I'll accept it and move on. I sure did like his name. I kept thinking of my Grandpa, Max. Both Max and Grandpa probably would have been good friends. Maybe there was even some spiritual connection. But, I'm retired, I don't have to think that deep.

By now, the morning had dragged on a little too much. Max had to get home, and I still had to walk back home, through the park, looking for those white tail deer. Max and I exchanged phone numbers, and I'm sure we'll get together sometime. Maybe we'll become friends. Who knows?

WHAT IF – Zak wouldn't have forgotten the milk?

Zak's Joyride of a Lifetime

The Dilemma

The Fourth of July in My Town U.S.A. I wait all year for this day. I start counting down on the Fifth of July for the next Fourth of July! Is there a more festive National Holiday? I don't think so. This year had a little twist to it though. Just my luck.

"Zak, I made your doctor's appointment for next Monday, July 1. Put the date on your calendar. It's at 9:30 in the morning, in his office downtown. They said not to eat anything for 12 hours. You can drink water but that's it."

"Yes, dear. Thank you. That was sweet of you." I'd been waiting for that; I wasn't in any hurry.

Now it's noon on July 1, and I just got back from Doc Johnson's office. I was still having stomach trouble and thought maybe I should have it investigated. It's been going on way too long. Doc said, "Zak, I don't have a crystal ball, and I'm not sure what your problem is. Everything I check seems normal. When you get back after the Fourth, from your two-week trip up north, we should run some tests, just to be on the safe side. I don't think it's anything serious, but we've got to keep an eye on it."

"Tanya, I'm not sure I want to go up to my brother's place after the Fourth." Doc Johnson took the wind out of my sails.

"Why not? You always love fishing with Chuck. You look forward to it every year." Tanya could be encouraging, at times. I know she was trying her best to make me feel better.

"Yeah, I do, but Doc wants to run some tests on me, and I'm not sure I want to wait two weeks. I'm a little concerned." Actually, I was more than concerned, I was downright worried.

"What did Doc say?" I know Tanya didn't totally believe me, she wanted to hear his opinion. She had that questioning look on her face.

"He says to go fishing, take a little pill twice a day, and everything should be fine. I don't like the words, 'should be fine.' They worry me." As much as I enjoy the Fourth of July, this one has somewhat of a damper on it. I'm not sure a hot dog and a beer will taste the same.

The Buildup

The July Fourth car show has an incredible mix of cars and trucks. Classics, hot rods, customs, stock—every make, every style, every color, just about anything you could imagine. It may only last a day, but it's a car guy's paradise, and I'm a car guy. It's as close to heaven as I can get, even with my stomach issues.

Over on Main Street, they have bed races—what a hoot those are. At four in the afternoon they start the parade, right down Main Street; then after dark there's the fireworks. Wherever you walk in my town you see homes dressed in red, white, and blue, with cookouts in just about every backyard. Who could ask for more, or better yet, who would want more?

Last year, the Fourth dawned to a bright sunny day that hit 102 degrees. Half, to three quarters of the old car owners didn't bring out their cars, it was a total bummer. The bed races also suffered from a lack of runners. Nobody over 25 even ran. This morning I woke up to a beautiful day. It was 75 and sunny, not a cloud in the sky, and no rain in the forecast for a week. The alarm was set for 6:30 a.m., and I was out of bed at quarter after. What could stop me now?

Tanya and I had the kind of discussion that most couples married 45 years would have at 6:15 in the morning, especially on a day off. We did some bantering back and forth and she decided that I'd pick her up at 10:30 a.m.. I decided it would be a good time to take my first little pill that Doc Johnson gave me. This was going to be a glorious day no matter what. That's what I thought anyway, was I in for a surprise.

Watching the old cars line up and enter the show grounds is always a thrill. There are young guys, old guys, happy kids, neat cars, jalopies, and everything in between. Everybody's getting along so well. These guys really seem to know the secret to coexisting, at least on the Fourth. It started me thinking about Max. He's a young guy, a nice guy with a family. He likes people. He has that neat bumper sticker on his station wagon about coexisting. I wondered if he ever came to the show. This may be the perfect time to find out. I decided it was time for that first phone call.

"Morning, Max. This is Zak, the guy from the grocery store express lane. The guy who lived up in New York City." The minute Max answered the phone I wondered how I could have been so dumb. How could I call a guy 8-inches taller and 60 pounds heavier than me, and about 40 years younger, and do it at 8:30 in the morning on the Fourth of July? I guess, as they say, 'stupid is as stupid does.'

"Morning, Zak. What's up? What in the world are you calling me for? It's just 8:30 in the morning." Well he didn't hang up, so I had to go on.

"Well, Max, this may seem like a dumb question, but I was wondering if you and your family ever come over to the car show on the Fourth? I'm over here now with all the families, and I thought of you and your kids." Yep! Stupid is as stupid does.

"Good grief. Yes! We've been doing the car show since we moved here three years ago. We love it. As a matter of fact, I was just getting my old pick-up truck ready to take over to the show." Max sounded happy.

"What?" I sounded confused.

"You heard me! Shirley and I were up late last night getting it all cleaned up. I'm running way behind schedule, having two young daughters can really slow things down. I wasn't sure how I was going to get both the truck and the family over to the show. You ever drive an old pick-up truck?" Max didn't know who he was talking to.

"Heck, yeah, I did. Back in high school, my uncle Ted had a '40 Ford pick-up truck out at his farm. During my junior and senior years in high school, he'd let me drive it into town for supplies during summer vacation." Those are the days a car guy never forgets.

Sometimes things happen that are so far out of the realm of possibilities all you can do is shrug your shoulders. This was one of those events. After talking with Max for about three minutes, he decided that I should drive his old truck from his place to the car show. Because I had driven my uncle Ted's old truck back and forth to town 50 years ago, Max thought I was his guy. Maybe I wasn't so stupid.

"What about Shirley, can't she drive it?" I had to ask.

"Shirley, drive the '41 pick-up truck, now that's a hoot. She's not even that interested in riding in it. She says it's not a Volvo." My lucky day.

The Pick-Up

Max picked me up at the show grounds, and we drove over to his place so I could get familiar with the truck. "Max, how in the world did you ever get ahold of this gorgeous old truck?" I was stunned.

"It's been in my family since it was new, and it's a long, long, long story. Let's just say there weren't a lot of male offspring in my family history. My uncle Joe had a farm, and I used to visit him often. When I was 14, he'd let me drive this thing around the farm. Joe knew I loved it, so he stipulated in his will that I'd get the truck if, and when, I graduated from college. He was a stickler for education. He died in 2010, and the truck was put into heated storage. I graduated, and the rest is history." That was my kind of history.

It's a 1941 Chevrolet, all original, half-ton pick-up truck. There were a few little dings in the bed, and some of the chrome was dull, but that was about it. It had just 37,267 miles on it. It's absolutely beautiful, and he's letting me drive it. Hope I'm up to the task.

I left his house driving the old truck and feeling on top of the world. It reminded me of driving my uncle Ted's old '40 Ford pick-up 50 years ago, what a great feeling, and then the unexpected.

"Max, I don't know what happened. I was just sitting here in line waiting to get up to the show entrance, and all of a sudden, it just died. I tried starting it. The battery's fine, but it won't start."

Max had that 'deer in the headlights' look. "Oh, crap. I forgot to fill it up yesterday, with all the running around to get it ready, I completely forgot to get gas. It must be empty; I'm getting almost as forgetful as you."

We were stuck in line behind six cars waiting to get into the show. We had to push the pick-up over to the side and find some gas. The Chevy dealer had a tank out back, so we borrowed a five-gallon gas can, and after about 10 minutes we were back in line. It seemed more like an eternity to us. 10 cars got in before us, but now we were actually driving the beauty into the show grounds.

Max was sitting in the cab right next to me waving at folks. I was driving right past hundreds of smiling people, and row after row of incredible vehicles. I was amazed with the turn of events. It took a lot of coaxing to get Max to calm down over the gas thing, I tried to assure him being 10 cars behind was no big deal. I reminded him we had all day, and everything would be fine, at least I hoped it would be. Little did I know at that time.

The Surprise

It was a huge surprise to both of us when we found out this was the 100th anniversary of the local Chevrolet dealer where the show was being held. This year also happened to be the 75th anniversary of their car show. It started back on July 4, 1941.

"Zak, when you called me this morning did you know this was the 75th anniversary of the car show. Are you sure I didn't tell you about my 75-year-old pick-up truck the other day? Have you been setting me up?"

"Max, I had no idea, and, no, you never mentioned anything about your beautiful old truck, but you should have. And, why would I set you up?" I didn't understand his question, but by this time, I was really getting to enjoy Max. The thought of Tanya meeting his whole family was getting exciting. I knew Tanya would enjoy it.

Then Max went on, "Well Zak, the judges here just told me that we brought in the 10,000th vehicle to enter the show since 1941. If we hadn't run out of gas when we did, we'd have been vehicle number

9,990. I'm not sure I believe in miracles, but this may have been one."

"Max, I believe in them, but I don't know if this qualifies. However, the odds of this must be 50 million to one. Running out of gas might have been the luckiest thing that's happened to you in years." I was thrilled with the turn of events.

Max's Grandpa bought the truck at this same Chevy dealership 75 years ago, on Monday, July 7, 1941. It was almost too much to comprehend. Max and his family became the unofficial 'Royal Family' for the day. Tanya and I got to tag along, and Tanya was thrilled with meeting his two daughters.

"Zak, the parade committee wants Shirley, the girls and me to ride in the back of the pick-up. They want us to be close to the beginning of the parade. They'll give the girls candy to toss out, and they said they'd decorate the truck a little. Would you and Tanya like to drive the truck? Think your stomach can handle it?"

It took me less than a second, "Whose stomach you talking about? Do I think I can handle it? Toss me the keys and get ready." I may have been getting a little arrogant, but I thought 'why not, I'm retired, I can handle this.' I drove with Tanya at my side. She was actually enjoying this. Max and his family rode in the bed on lawn chairs as the 'King and his Royal Family.'

The parade committee had decorated the sides all the way around with those red, white, and blue buntings, the kind you see on porch railings. The truck looked fantastic. They had a 3-foot by 5-foot USA flag mounted on the drivers' side front corner of the bed, and a 3-foot by 5-foot State flag mounted on the passenger front corner. Max and Shirley had small flags to wave, and the girls were given six pails of little candies to toss.

The Fun Begins

We were put in the third spot in the parade. The mayor and his wife were in the first spot and we were just behind the local VFW group. I started calling the truck Old Betsy, and when I started her up, for some reason she backfired.

"Max, what gives? What did I do wrong? Did I screw something up?" My stomach started talking to me for the first time.

"Zak, you didn't screw anything up. There must be something in the gas we put in, maybe there was some water in it." I should have thought of that.

Well, when the VFW guys heard the backfire, they thought it was their signal to do the 21-gun salute. They were all running around getting their guns set, and when they all got in line they started firing. Seven guns, three shots each. No one had any idea about what was going on, but all the spectators were applauding.

"Zak, now what did you do?" That's what Tanya asked me after the guns went off and she got her composure back.

"Tanya, I have no clue. All I know is Old Betsy sure started something."

That wasn't so bad, but then the fella driving the white, totally restored, 1959 Cadillac convertible up in the front spot thought that was his signal to start driving. That wasn't even so bad; however, our Mayor and his wife were on the sides of the road shaking hands, doing those political things politicians do. They had to run a block and a half to catch up to the Cadillac. Our Mayor probably picked up some votes for that escapade. People were cheering and clapping.

"Zak, what just happened? Shirley, the girls, and I are sitting here looking out the back and heard all the noise. People are laughing and smiling and waving at us. What's up?" This was getting to be fun.

"Max, no sweat, everything's under control. I guess Old Betsy just wanted us to know she's alive. Hold on and have fun."

The parade route was two miles long, right down main street. The crowds were incredible, and the weather was perfect. Then, at about the one-mile mark, we had to wait five minutes for the cross traffic on State Highway 51. I turned Old Betsy off to cool the engine down a little while we sat it out. Started her up, and sure enough, she had to backfire again. What luck?

Well, we were two units in front of four officers from our police academy. They each had an extremely well trained, perfectly behaved, beautiful, but scary looking, drug sniffing German Shepherd. Unfortunately, the dogs heard the backfire, thought it was a gun shot and took off sniffing for drugs. Up and down both sides of the street, two on each side, sniffing kids candy bags, sniffing family coolers and picnic baskets. They went about sniffing people and barking and barking and sniffing people. The officers were totally embarrassed and finally got their dogs settled down and back in line. It was an incredible sight to watch.

"Zak, what the heck just happened? What's with the dogs? Shirley, the girls, and I are having a ball. People are running up to the back of the truck congratulating us and telling us they never had so much fun at a parade. How'd you do that?"

"Max, I'm doing my thing, Old Betsy's doing her thing, Tanya's riding shot-gun and having a grand time. You and your family should just enjoy."

I never had to take the truck out of first gear through the entire two-mile long parade. However, just before the two-mile mark, I noticed the temperature gauge starting to climb. I was able to control it somewhat by revving the engine a little. That seemed to help. But, right there, right in front of the judges' stand, it started steaming, with just over 200 yards to go.

"Max, I've got to shut Old Betsy down. We can't take a chance with the engine; we've got to let it cool off."

I had no choice but to turn it off. This was, after all, a 75-year-old classic that had survived without any major problems to this point. This was no time to mess with it.

Well, the committee started doing whatever a committee would do under the predicament. This person saying that, and that person saying this and then, out of nowhere, six of Max's football players came out of the crowd. The judges stand was where the bed races ended about an hour earlier, and his football players had been in the races. They didn't win anything, but they had a ball. They were dressed as female cheerleaders.

You can imagine the fun the crowd had with them. Six young, tough high school football jocks, all dressed up like young female cheerleaders. The guys started pushing the old pick-up—200 yards was nothing to those guys. It was amazing! The crowd started cheering, whistling, and clapping. Max stood up and started waving that big 3-foot by 5-foot American Flag. The girls stood up and started singing, "Happy Birthday, USA."

The Payoff

The Chevy dealer offered lifetime oil changes, and vehicle washes for the 10,000th vehicle. They also had a $10,000 pre-paid VISA card for the 10,000th vehicle. Max liked that! Considering it was a vehicle purchased from them 75 years earlier, they asked Max if he'd allow them to display the truck in their showroom all next winter. How could Max turn that down.

"Max, I can't thank you enough for today's enjoyment. Up to now, all I've ever done here is walk around the grounds looking at the old cars, having a hot dog and beer, and feeling a little stupid. Now, I still may be a little stupid, but I feel like a celebrity. Tanya's glowing, and your daughters are both holding her hands. I'm speechless!"

"Well, Zak. It has been fun, and a darn nice day. I'm glad we met that day in the express lane." Me too.

Tanya and I took our two-week trip up north, to see my brother. I spent a lot of time fishing and thinking about my stomach. We got home, and I went back to Doc Johnson. They ran some tests, and some levels are off a little. Doc says he's not too worried, and neither should I be. However, he's not in my shoes.

He says it's a wait and see situation. Happy days.

P.S. – It's now December 20th, and Doc. Johnson has me on some kind of stomach medication. Apparently, everything turned out ok, but I have to stay away from Brandy, Lemons, Chocolate, Express Lanes, and ladies in yellow spandex.

WHAT IF – *Zak had been afraid to call Max?*

My Dear Friend -

All Alone

My folks and his folks knew each other for years before I was born.

He and I were of different ethnic backgrounds, but that wasn't the real problem. The real problem was that I always thought he was so much better than me. Maybe it was just my problem. Whatever the case, it was a real problem for me when I was growing up. He was a little older than I was. I guess that means I knew him ever since the day I was born.

My earliest recollection of my friend was in kindergarten. My mom took me to school that first day, and at recess I ran home. It was only three blocks, and I thought Mom would be glad to see me. Boy was I in for a surprise. Good old Mom took me right back. I think I cried, and my feelings were crushed. How could she do that to me? I thought I was the apple of her eye.

That first day of kindergarten was the beginning of a lifetime of learning that it really wasn't all about me at all. There was a whole lot more to this life than just me. That was a tough lesson for me to learn. I think I'm still learning.

I was incredibly miserable that day. I had to introduce myself to the rest of the class, I thought it was dumb, because I already knew most of them. Then I had to take a nap, which I thought was even dumber, because all I wanted to do was play outside. My friend told me it would all be ok. It would work out fine, and we'd be going home in no time. He said that right after he helped our teacher put all the stuffed animals away. He was always the teacher's pet. That's the way it seemed to the rest of us.

I did like him though; he was hard not to like. He had such a pleasant disposition. However, there were times in kindergarten when I wasn't so sure about him. I sometimes wondered why he'd do what he was doing.

His kindness helped me get through kindergarten.

By the time I got to the third grade, I was beginning to understand him a little better. It wasn't that he was the teacher's pet, but that I always felt insecure whenever I was around him. I'm not sure why. Maybe it was because I didn't understand why he was always so nice to everybody, while I sometimes felt crabby. Sometimes I didn't want to talk to anybody, I'd just want to hide. We were, however, becoming better friends. I just couldn't help it. I'd smile at him and greet him wherever we'd meet.

"Hey, how are you doing? I noticed you were kind of hiding behind that tree when I walked past the other day. Were you hiding from me or what?" He asked me that with his eyebrows scrunched up and twisted.

"No, I wasn't hiding at all. I was just looking to see where the moss was growing and if there were any rabbit droppings. Why would I hide from you anyway?" My dumb response, while I was standing on one foot looking down at the ground.

"I'm not sure, but sometimes you don't seem happy." He knew me pretty well, all he had to do was look at my face.

"I guess, but you always seem so darn happy, and sometimes I feel so crummy. I'd like to be more like you." I straightened up on both feet and tried to smile.

"Well just give it a try. It's not that hard." That's what he said with a huge smile, it sounded like a good idea to me.

I spent the next few years trying to emulate him. Trying to be a little nicer, and a little less crabby. I think it was working. I'd wake up in the morning with a smile on my face, at least half the time. By the sixth grade, I stopped trying to hide from people, and I was feeling a little more secure. I was doing pretty good in school by that time. I always passed all my classes, sometimes just barely, but I always passed.

My friend and I had a lot of mutual buddies. We played all the different sports together. There were all kinds of pickup games around the neighborhood. No one could beat us at two against two touch football. We were the best there ever was, at least in our neighborhood. I enjoyed those times together, that's when I'd forget about how smart he was. I'd feel his equal, at least on the football field.

Mom was thrilled. She really did like his folks. I was glad. Mom knew his mother ever since she was a little girl. They didn't go to school together, but they lived in the same small town. They'd see each other at church sometimes on Sundays. They would talk about their families, their folks, what they should do about some problem or another, and they'd exchange recipes. They'd do the things moms would do. It always made me happy that my mom liked his mom so much.

By eighth grade, we were becoming better friends, although sometimes our friendship would get strained, but it always seemed to be my fault. He was always much smarter than I was, and, every once in a while, it made me feel dumb. There were times when he'd do so much better than me on an exam that I'd actually be envious, and I'd avoid him for days. He'd say hi, and I'd try to look busy or pretend I didn't hear him. He never pushed me for an answer; he had tons of patience with me. I didn't deserve it.

"Hey, you know we graduate next month, and I'm having a

little party. You want to come over?" I was thrilled that he invited me, but I didn't want to get too close.

"What? I didn't hear you." I tried to avoid him.

"I said, my parents are having an eighth grade graduation party. Do you want to come over?" He was hard to avoid, and he was so sincere.

"I'd like to, but my grandparents are having a party for me. Thanks anyway." That's the way it was with me in grade school. I liked him, but I was leery of getting too close to him.

He helped me get through grade school. He pushed me without my even knowing it. In my attempt to be more like my friend, I was learning.

In our freshman year of high school, I got to know him much better. Our homeroom desks were right next to each other. I always figured Mom had something to do with that. She worked in the front office and had lots of pull. That's when he and I started discussing things. Some topics were pretty deep, and some were just guy things. It was becoming a better friendship.

He taught me a lot about how things should really be, and not necessarily how they were. I learned a lot from him that year. Sometimes, though, it was hard to comprehend what he was talking about. He could get pretty philosophical about things and life. He had a lot of good ideas for living. I tried my best to remember what he'd say, and I'd take notes. Freshman year was a good year. I stopped thinking I was just some crabby, dumb kid.

Sophomore year was the time I started becoming much more outgoing. I kept trying to be more like my friend. He had a way about him. He was always popular, even the teachers admired him, that's when I'd get jealous. Sometimes I'd avoid him for a day or two, and once I even faked stomach cramps for two days. Mom took me to see our family doctor who determined my problem was "just in his head." Needless to say, I was back in school on the third day. Good old mom, she could see right through me.

During junior year, we drifted apart a bit. I got my driver's license, he never wanted to drive. He was becoming more scholarly than I was, and now I was really beginning to notice it. Teachers would make comments like, "Why can't you be more like your good friend over there?" Our principal even called my parents into a special meeting to try and get them to hire my friend as my tutor. That got under my skin quite a bit. I was a C or B student, and my friend was always an A+ student. He always helped me study, and if I was falling behind, he'd try to warn me.

One of our typical conversations was something like:

"How's your English assignment coming along? You know the book report is due soon. Have you even read the book?" His head was looking down at his desk and he peered over the top of his glasses. He knew I didn't.

"Huh, I didn't hear anything about any homework or book report. When did she give us that? When is it due?" I was getting great at playing dumb.

"It was right at the end of the class, just before the bell rang. You did hear the bell, didn't you? I can't believe you'd miss the bell. You're always in such a hurry to get out of here." He knew me well. Maybe too well.

"I think I was looking at Sally Jane when the bell rang. Could you give me a clue on what Miss Jenkins said? What book was I supposed to read?" I may have been trying his patience.

"The book is Moby Dick, and I'm not helping you. You've got

to do this on your own. And don't forget, homework is due to-morrow for seventh period, and the book report is due next week Friday." He got up from his desk and closed his book with a rather loud thud. Maybe he cared too much.

"No problem. I'll do the homework right after I watch some TV tonight, and the book report is a cinch. How hard can it be to read about a fish? Don't worry about it." Looking back, I'm not sure why he had so much patience with me.

That's how many of our conversations went through our junior and senior years. The only things that changed during those years were the topics. Girls, cars, smoking, drinking, and skipping out of school—all the crazy things I would talk about. He and I were never on the same page on any of those topics, but he'd always listen and smile.

Never too judgmental, not my friend.

He'd always talk things over with me. He'd give me his thoughts on any subject I wanted to talk about. Even though he was so much smarter than I was, he never held it over my head. He was, as they say, down to earth.

I tried to listen and pay attention to him, but sometimes I'd figure, oh, what does he really know about that? Like, I never saw him change a sparkplug in a '52 Chevy. I never saw him take a deep drag off a Lucky Strike cigarette. I never even saw him change a flat tire. He probably could have. Probably three times faster than I could, but I never saw it.

No matter all the differences between us, we were becoming good friends. After all, I'd known him my whole life.

He helped me get through high school. I think it was his com-plete confidence and faith in me. He always seemed to know when

I had my doubts, was down and out, or maybe I was becoming too cocky or arrogant. He kept me on track.

We started college together. That's when I probably drifted away from him more than he liked. It seemed we were going our separate ways. He wasn't very happy about it. Maybe I was getting a little too big for my britches.

He'd ask me things like:

"Say, did you hear Mr. Fitzpatrick broke his leg last week? Some of us guys are going over to help him with his yardwork Saturday. Want to join us?" He called me on the phone just to ask me. He wasn't giving up on me.

"Geez, I'd love to, but I've got to wash and wax my car. I'm going cruising with the guys Saturday night. You know, up and down the Avenue, looking for chicks. You should come along with us some night. Nah, it's probably not your thing." I was a jerk for saying that, but it was done.

Or:

"By the way, this weekend they're having a fundraising car wash for that family who had the fire last week. Sounds like fun. You want to help? Should I pick you up?" He actually sounded sincere, like I might really help.

"Geez, I'd love to, but I think I'm busy with some of the other guys. Bill mentioned something about going fishing and camping up at the lake this weekend. Thanks for the invite, though. I sure would have enjoyed it." I should have listened to him, that would have been a good time for me to change my attitude. Maybe I would have become a little less self-centered. Who knows?

That's the way it went on and off through college. We did remain friends through it all, we just had very different ideas. Looking back on it now, he always was my good friend, I just didn't realize it at the time. College is an awkward age, you're not a kid, and you're not really an adult. My friend always seemed more like an adult than the rest of us.

Thinking back, I guess I always was somewhat jealous of him, but I also admired him. I also knew I was concerned about losing his friendship. I don't really know why, maybe I would have felt lost without him. Maybe my friend kept me a little more stable. I just know I kept him as a good friend. Lucky for me.

He helped me get through college. Like he'd been doing my whole life. He wasn't going to let me slip away.

After college, I really did drift away from him. I got married, started a family, was in over my head in a lot of things, and I didn't even know it. I heard he became a teacher, but not just any teacher, he became an actual scholar. I wasn't at all surprised. People would meet in large groups just to hear him talk, and to get his advice. He was becoming extremely popular, and very much in demand. Knowing we were good friends always meant a lot to me, even though I'd hardly ever see him.

Occasionally, we'd talk on the phone, something like:

"I'm giving a seminar on dealing with family life and raising children next Sunday afternoon. Want to come over? I can get you in for free." My dear good friend just wouldn't stop asking. By this time his voice had gotten much deeper, he sounded like someone you'd love to listen to for hours.

"Sure, I'd love to, but my wife and I are getting along wonderfully, and the kids, well, they're not a problem. You know how kids are, they like to complain, it just seems to be in their nature. We're all doing fine. Good luck with the seminar though. I'm sure there's plenty of folks that could use your help." I think I was sitting in my recliner having a beer and some chips when he called.

Or:

"Geez, I haven't seen you in quite a while. Why don't you stop by my place on Sunday? We can hash over the old days. How about it? I'd really like to talk to you. It's been a long time, and I miss hearing from you." Miss me? How lucky could a guy get; I wish I would have realized it at the time.

"Sure, I'd love to. But this Sunday is the big game. You know we're in the playoffs. I know you don't follow them as much as I do, but some of the guys are having a heck of a party down in Larry's basement. You ought to stop by." Was I was brushing him off? Was I still too self-centered? Was I really a jerk?

Well, we did get together occasionally. We always had a grand time when we did. After all, I knew him my whole life. He knew all the old gang. He knew all my pros and cons. He knew all about my family. He seemed to know all my history. I did get to know his mom pretty well. She was the sweetest lady I've ever known, next to my mom, of course. I knew his stepfather somewhat. I'd see all three of them together on occasion.

I think some of the best times we had over all those years were the rare times it was just the two of us. We could talk forever. He never seemed to judge me or tire of me. I always knew he was totally honest with me, even when he told me things I really didn't want to hear. Sometimes he'd holler at me, sometimes he'd speak quietly, and sometimes he'd just listen. Luckily, a lot of what he said stayed with me, even if it was in my subconscious. I sure had a lot to learn from him.

I know he traveled the world over and was fluent in at least four languages. Once in a while, I'd get a message from him from the strangest place, very often predicting something that was about to happen. I'd keep tabs on the news and sure enough, he'd be right. I was never surprised.

I hadn't seen him in quite a while, and I was feeling kind of low, so I went to see him the other day.

He was gone, but a mutual friend was there. He explained what happened to my friend.

I was mortified, and I cried.

While he was in some far-off country, he was crucified.

His teachings offended some of the locals, so they took some long nails and they nailed his hands and feet onto an old wooden cross, and they crucified him. First, they placed a homemade crown made from some thorny tree on his head. Then, they made him carry his cross up a hill, with a little help from a total stranger.

They left my Friend there to die. Alone on an old wooden cross.

You know what He did?

He forgave them.

Yep, that's exactly what He did. My Good Friend forgave. He forgave me for not visiting often enough in the past. What I do now is up to me.

He left me a note telling me that if I wanted to, I could see Him again. He said it was up to me. He said there were many rooms where He was going. He wrote in the note that if I thought about Him often enough, visited Him frequently, and even talked to Him occasionally, it would help me a great deal.

In the note, He wrote down what was going to happen to Him, the exact place, the exact time, and exactly how it was all going to go down, right down to the final hour. He knew the future. The only person who ever has. He still let it happen. He could have stopped it, but He let it happen.

He said it was for everybody, can you believe that?

He can help me with my future.

Guaranteed!

Unlike all of the uncontrollable twists of fate that have happened in my life, and will continue to happen, the only thing I have complete and total control over is where my Soul will spend Eternity.

It's all up to me.

P.S. – My Best Friend is available for anyone! All you have to do is ask.

WHAT IF – My Best Friend had not died on the cross?

Epilogue

After reading the 12 short stories, you'll have a better understanding as to what a Twist of Fate can do.

The first 11 stories are fictional but could very well be something that may have happened in your life.

Just imagine for a moment, that the stop light in front of you turned red at the instant you got to it and you were held up for exactly one minute. Then when you arrived at the shopping center that front row parking space you were going to enter (you always managed to get that first spot)—well just because you were one minute late—someone got there first, oh shucks. Now you had to park in the back row and walk all the way up to the store, and then, all the way back to your car after shopping—oh shucks, again.

But wait a minute—you found that to be good exercise, it was actually fun to do. You started doing it on a regular basis, you were getting excited, walking was fun. All of a sudden, you became a walker. You lost 25 pounds. Life was great again—holy cow—this was great. You lived 15 years longer.

All because you hit one stop light on red, rather than green. A twist of fate?

How about this...

It's a beautiful day and you're on vacation in the Great Smoky Mountains, you happen to sprain your ankle slipping on the bathroom rug—oh shucks. You were supposed to be going on a group hike up along one of the difficult sections of the Appalachian Trail, but now you can't. Well I'll let you finish the scenario your way—but I was going to say, now you were stuck at the resort and out of boredom you bought the winning multi-million-dollar lottery ticket, see what I mean? A twist of fate?

The 12th short story is a combination of fiction and real life. (The dialog is fiction; the theme is real life). It's my life, but maybe it could be your life also. Is that possible? Thinking back over my lifetime, I've spent a lot of the time being self-centered, being a jerk. I didn't realize it at the time, I was just being me, but thankfully my Best Friend never ignored me. He never gave up on me. He helped me then and He's helping me now.

We have absolutely no control over so much of our lives and we don't even realize it. You know the only thing we have complete and total control over is our soul, and it's destiny.

My Best Friend can help with that.